SONG FOR OLIVIA

MARUCHI MENDEZ

Library of Congress Control Number: 2022937098

ISBN: 9798985194630

Printed in the United States of America

23 24 25 26 27 5 4 3 2 1

When I think of all the women in my life who have influenced me and loved me, I am charged and refueled throughout life's journey. This journey in which I have received, taken, given, bargained, and been penalized. In any way and form—it has been lived to the fullest, and made me who I am. The women in my family, young and old, have been and presently are the strongest beings I know. I dedicate this book to my sisters, especially Olga who is no longer by my side. A big thanks to Ray, Josh, and Omer, who have believed in me and encouraged me to write this story which has been nine years in the making—and to my own Sunshine Tribe, for their love, support, and constant supply of kisses and eight second hugs. "We are joyful, vibrant, full of energy, and nothing can stop us."

Contents

CHAPTER 1: Havana, Cuba 1

CHAPTER 2: The Punishment 11

CHAPTER 3: *Gusanos* 17

CHAPTER 4: The New Beginning 29

CHAPTER 5: Hope 43

CHAPTER 6: The Lie 57

CHAPTER 7: The Truth 67

CHAPTER 8: *El Perro ya Llegó* 79

CHAPTER 9: The Secret 83

CHAPTER 10: Where Do the Ducks Go? 89

CHAPTER 11: Malaria 101

CHAPTER 12: The Ring 109

CHAPTER 13: *Liebestraum* (Love Dream) 117

CHAPTER 14: The Competition 125

CHAPTER 15: The Crisis 137

CHAPTER 16: Till Death Do Us Part 145

CHAPTER 17: Caught 153

CHAPTER 18: Courage 163

CHAPTER 19: The Visitor 169

CHAPTER 20: Love Wins 183

CHAPTER 21: The Aftermath 193

CHAPTER 22: The Ocean 203

1

Havana, Cuba

My mother never told me that she loved me until she was about to die. Then again, she never liked me much. I was what she would call "incorrigible." Bone-deep incorrigible, and I made sure to play the part. As the youngest of three sisters, I figured her patience had run out by the time I was born. Stories of her daylong labor, and me making everyone wait until 11:56 p.m. to finally enter this world—and on a Friday the 13th—sealed my reputation as a difficult child. It didn't help that during the pregnancy, her mother, who was her best friend, had died. This sank my mom into deep mourning that would last for years.

So we didn't have a good start.

Fortunately, I had my oldest sister, Olivia, who was four years older than I was and was my guardian angel. Every time I got in trouble or looked up in despair, her eyes were there. She knew how to soothe me and protect me like a mother would. We were also the house pranksters, and our pranks, which were aimed at my middle sister, Lucia, would not go unpunished. But even then, as we sat for hours of punishment, I felt fortunate to be her sister, and the punishment was more like bonding.

Our Mother used to sit us face-to-face when we did something to Lucia and force us to hug and say we were sorry. Then we had to continue looking at each other for what seemed to be an eternity. The hugging always puzzled me because my mother wasn't what you would call a hugger. I can only remember a handful of hugs from her in my entire life. Olivia, on the other hand, had the warmest hugs, and I used to cuddle against her chest and put my hands around her waist to get one. Lucia was very kind and would forgive us. The first hugs during the punishment were fake and meant to appease my mother. But afterwards her methods worked; we all hugged several times, and I sobbed for forgiveness. When our mother would release us from our punishment, Olivia would always whisper in my ear:

"We mustn't do this again." But that didn't last long.

We were three sisters: Olivia, the oldest; Lucia, the middle one; and me, Maria Josefa de Jesus, named after the Sacred Family and my recently deceased grandmother. Luckily, I was later given the nickname of Mary Jo at Moss Lake Summer Camp in upstate New York, and my sisters called me Mari at home. There was a lot of mystery surrounding my grandmother's life and death, and many questions went unanswered, but in time I came to understand that our names of Mary, Joseph, and Jesus had nothing to do with holiness. To the contrary, she had a very tumultuous love life, so we shared a bond through namesake, and that suited me just fine.

Growing up Enriqueta's daughter in Havana, Cuba, during the 1950s wasn't easy. My mom used to stand us in front of her and tell us to never challenge her words and to obey without question. "If I say the sun is purple, then it is purple," she would say in anger. I resisted her every time. My sisters, on the other hand just stood there, half-laughing and half-afraid to make her angry. When she said *y punto*, which means "period," the conversation was over. We could see the first signs of her anger when she clenched her fist and bit her tongue. She never hit us or screamed. She just squeezed our arms and pinched them, and then she whipped us with her tongue.

The words came out low, slow, and deliberately crafted to plunge us into that deep sea of guilt and shame where she apparently never spent a day. In my mind, she was perfect, and doing exactly what she told us would earn us her love and admiration. That was all I wanted.

My mom, Enriqueta Mendiola, was a devout Catholic and the daughter of a judge in the Supreme Court of Cuba and his wife, Maria Josefa, 20 years younger. She was an only child, raised by an American governess, and she spoke fluent English and French. Her mother was a socialite and something of a hypochondriac. She would take Enriqueta to the doctor often and bathed her in salt and iodine to deliver the benefits of the ocean—hence my mother's fascination with chemistry. Her own mother's beauty was apparent in all the photos we had seen, and they loved traveling with the governess. My mother told us tales of visiting the Fairchilds and taking walks in their sumptuous gardens. It was said that Maria Josefa, my grandmother, had an affair with an Italian painter that she met during her travels. Although my mom didn't speak of it, I overheard my aunt in a conversation.

My mom was a gifted student and attended La Universidad de la Habana, where she obtained master's degrees in music and in chemistry (go figure). It was at the university that she met my father, Lorenzo Solano, who was completing his finance and accounting degrees. Upon graduating, they married when she was in her mid-30s. She had Olivia nine months later, Lucia 10 months after that, and then me—her "accident"—4 years later. After her mother's death and the depression that followed, she said that it was her three daughters that gave her a purpose to continue in life. I tested her limits, constantly wanting her love and attention, when all along she was doing the best she could as her mother had done before her. She spent every minute of our childhood making sure we became well-rounded, refined, and cultured ladies. She walked the walk and was the strongest, most determined human being I knew.

We grew up in revolutionary pre-Castro Havana amid the fighting in the mountains and the bombs going off in the city. Assassination attempts (some successful) on President Batista's government officials were in the news every day. My father, Lorenzo Solano, was a cabinet member of the Batista government, and in the last two years we spent in Havana, bodyguards waited for us outside our school. Inside our home, our parents tried to ignore the situation. Money was abundant, and we continued eating off of fine English bone china and drinking from Baccarat stemware.

Our long day would start with sweet *café con leche* and warm, toasted, buttered Cuban bread. I never wanted to go to school and would sit at the edge of my bed complaining while the nanny laced up my saddle shoes. This caused my sisters to be late to school more often than not. Our chauffeur-bodyguard drove us and our heavy leather book bags in a big, black government car to our school, Las Ursulinas. This was an all-girls school run by the Ursuline nuns, or mothers, as we called them. Our bags were bursting at the seams, and the trunk of the car contained our gear for the rest of the day. When school would finish at 4 p.m., the car was there waiting. The trunk would open, and another book bag would appear to take the place of the heavy leather one. The chauffeur would smile at us with pity standing by the car as he handed us the new bags with music composition books about solfège, Czerny, and Hanon, and, depending on the day, our ballet gear. Off we went to the International Conservatory of Music, run by Maria Jones de Castro (no relation to Fidel). There, we continued the drill of growing up as Enriqueta's daughters. Elizabeth Lincoln Otis's *An "If" for Girls* couldn't hold a candle to the aspirations she had for us. Our courses included piano, *solfège,* music harmony, music history, singing, ballet, and dance. We also attended a finishing school known as Instituto de Arte e Idiomas, where we learned to master English with Miss Harriet Patterson and took French lessons with Madame Yolande Pelloutier. We were taught correct manners, including body posture, etiquette, and all the refinement expected of the girls in our society. There was also the Lyceum, which we attended on Saturdays for flower arrangement classes, table etiquette, sewing, and, my favorite, cooking. Once a year, we would compete in the flower arrangement competition, and, Olivia, who was born with the gift of good taste, would always win first prize. Saturday afternoons my sisters took horseback riding at El Picadero Hipico. I was too young, my mother said, and wasn't ready.

***

"Mari, wake up. We're going to be late."

Olivia came to Mari's aid. "Get up Mari! We're going downstairs for breakfast, and you're still in your pajamas. I'm going to get really mad."

The morning started off as usual—me making my sisters wait. Little did I know that many things were about to change.

At school, Sister Rose kept scolding me to the ridiculous tune of, "Stop looking out the window, Maria Josefa. What are you looking at, Maria Josefa?"

Finally, I couldn't take it anymore and answered back.

"I'm looking for God, but all I see are birds."

Quickly she came and grabbed my arm and my chair. She took me to the corner of the classroom where I sat facing the wall and counting the ants until Sister Margarita rang the bell.

That afternoon at the conservatory, I hid from my piano teacher and went to play hopscotch a block away with some neighbor girls. It caused so much commotion that the entire conservatory came looking for me. I could hear their voices calling my name, but by the time I came back, class was over, much to my relief.

By the time we got home, my mother had received the call from my piano teacher. She sent me straight up to my room, and I wasn't allowed to come down for dinner. Thankfully, I had stashed Cuban crackers and a couple of Baby Ruths inside one of my drawers, which came in handy as always. After dinner, my mother came up.

"What am I going to do with you? You defy everyone."

I wanted her to give up on me and piano lessons. You see, my sister Olivia played the piano like an angel. She played Rachmaninoff's "Bells of Moscow" like no one else. Lucia, on the other hand, loved to compose and had an incredible musical ear. There was nothing she couldn't play. I decided that it was easier for me to say, "I don't like piano," than sit with my mother, also a good pianist, and practice during our "free" time. Being the rebel I was, I stood my ground for many years by claiming lack of talent and lack of interest. I regret to this day having wasted the opportunity to master this beautiful instrument, which I actually did love.

One more time I told her, "I hate piano—I don't want to play piano." Then suddenly it dawned on me. "I want singing lessons." And that would lead to voice lessons with one of the best opera singers in Cuba.

The day after my scolding, I faked a stomachache and stayed home from school. That afternoon, I decided to go into the kitchen, which our mother had forbidden us from doing. I loved the smells of the kitchen and the gossip of the servants. Margot, who ran our kitchen, would let me peel potatoes and lick the spoons of the dessert she was making. My mother came home and caught me, spoon in hand.

"Go upstairs to your room right now, and I'll speak to you later."

"Why?" I asked defiantly. "There's nothing wrong with me staying here."

"Because I say so."

Olivia, who had joined me in the kitchen, was nervous but still stood up for me.

"She's bored, Mami. She wants to learn how to cook."

"Olivia, I said no. *Punto.*"

I went upstairs, and Olivia followed me. Being furious at my mother wasn't good for anyone. My mom would never budge, and I wouldn't either. My mom followed us upstairs as Olivia tried to calm me.

"Just stay quiet and don't talk back to her." She knew how small things could escalate with my mom and me.

"Why does she hate me so much? She doesn't let me do anything! I wasn't disrespectful, I just answered her question." By then I was sobbing.

"That's not true Mari, she loves you very much. We all do. You have to control yourself and not answer back."

Olivia was the only person that I listened to. She was my idol. Olivia was strong, charismatic, and the apple of my father's eye. She had him wrapped around her finger. His pride for her was undeniable, and rightfully so. Since she was small, she had had a strong sense of fashion and had inherited my mother's good eye and taste for decoration and finer things. She was an accomplished concert pianist and an excellent ballerina at the age of 14, which pleased my mom.

Lucia, on the other hand, had health problems and was more delicate and sensitive. A music prodigy, she composed from the age of six and was my mother's pride and joy. I loved her dearly. Her sensitivity was apparent in everything she did. It was also the reason she would cry so easily. She was too fragile for us. By us, I mean Olivia and me. This is the reason that she clung to our mother. My mom would defend Lucia and protect her from our lack of patience and unkindness. Every time my mother would look at Lucia, I saw a special shine in her eyes. They were inseparable. Even as a teenager, my mother would sit with her and plead with her to eat. One day, the nanny was peeling her grapes and taking the seeds out for her. I asked my mother why no one peeled the grapes for me, and she answered, "Because you eat too much."

Olivia was so bothered by this that she sat next to Lucia and told her that the bread had ants and the grapes were sour. She was trying to avenge me, but my poor sister Lucia always fell for it and cried.

Our trips in the summer to Moss Lake Camp seemed to bring us closer together. There we had no piano, no one to peel our grapes, and no shoulder to cry on. We would fly from Havana and arrive in New York, where we were met by a camp counselor. There were only five girls from Cuba that attended the exclusive, girls-only Moss Lake Camp, and that included the three of us. The counselor would then escort us to Grand Central Station, where we would catch a train to upstate New York. The camp was located near the Canadian border and deep in the Adirondack Mountains by the edge of Big Moose Lake. We needed to wear wool jackets in the morning because the temperature was in the 30s. There we learned fencing, archery, tennis, horseback riding, canoeing, and sailing, among many other things. We also learned to be independent and away from Enriqueta's unbending rules. I attended junior camp, and my sisters went to senior camp. I was allowed to walk over and see them on Sundays after Mass. I would always see them together, smiling and talking to each other in a way that was completely different from their interactions in Cuba. Lucia would hang on every word that Olivia spoke, and Olivia treated Lucia with the same kindness that she would use for me. I realized at that early age that in Cuba, they were just competing over everything—the piano, the ballet, and my mother's attention.

I took from those months many warm memories that would make me look forward to going back the next year. My favorite was the train ride from New York to the pickup location near Lake Placid. We rode all night, and our seats turned into bunk beds. I would crack open the window nearest to me. The smell of the Adirondack conifer forest would fill my senses, and the slashing cold air invigorated me in a way that prevented sleep. In the early morning hours, our caboose would be disengaged and would remain until a bus from Moss Lake Camp would pick us up.

In August, when camp ended, my parents would pick us up and we would drive in a rented car back to Manhattan, where my mother did her shopping. I really looked forward to summers, and I remember dreading the strict routine that awaited us upon our return to our role as Enriqueta's daughters in Havana.

2

THE PUNISHMENT

It was Sunday, and my mother was still not speaking to me. We got dressed like on any other Sunday to go to Mass in the morning. Olivia helped me pick out my dress and shoes and combed my hair. I loved it when Olivia combed my hair and made my ponytail while I just sat at the dressing table. Sometimes she would put a hint of lipstick on me, and I felt very important.

"Olivia, why am I the only one with black hair?" I asked for the tenth time.

"I have no idea, Mari. I've told you that there are blondes and brunettes in both sides of the family. Don't forget that you look like Snow White with your white skin and straight, black hair."

I really wanted to look like Olivia. She was beautiful with her medium blonde hair and movie-star aura. Her skin had a velvet shine, and when she stepped out into the sun, there was a glow about her. Lucia had even lighter blonde hair and a natural tan. It was my grandmother Maria Josefa who had the straight, jet-black hair and that insipid skin as white as snow.

"You look like my mother," Mami would tell me. "Your skin is like porcelain, just like hers."

But I didn't want to look like her mother, either. I wanted to look like Olivia.

We went to Mass at St. Augustine's Catholic Church, where we listened to the homily of Father Espirelli. My father would always hand each of us a one-dollar bill for the offertory. That dollar was the happiest part of the week for Olivia, Lucia, and me. Placing that money in the collection basket taught us the joy of giving to others, and we have continued to do so. I sat between both of my sisters during Mass that day. Each Sunday we would watch how long people kneeled after communion to determine the degree of their sinful behavior. Then we would try to imagine stories in their life. Did they steal something or hurt someone? Maybe they lied a lot. My father used to get up right away. After taking our communion and kneeling in our pew, we sat on the bench, and Olivia put her arm around me while I hugged her waist. Lucia, on my other side, put her head on my shoulder. I felt warm and safe between them and free of sin.

That afternoon, my mother came to me and sat me down next to her.

"I have decided you will go to boarding school."

I craved adventure, so right away I responded. "Where would I go?"

"I'm not sure yet. We will find the right place for you."

"Will my sisters be going to boarding school also?"

"No, not them, Mari, only you."

I didn't even bother to ask why because it was obvious. The last two incidents had been too much, and she told me that there would be changes. Also, my sisters' social lives had become busier, and I was four years younger. They had moved up to high school and were becoming grown-ups, with dress fittings at the couturiere, endless shopping at El Encanto, and visits to hair salons. My mother relished all things *société*, but it was all boring to me, and I was getting in their way. So I pretended that I preferred to stay home.

That evening, I sat with my sister Olivia.

"Olivia, have you heard which boarding school I'm going to?" I asked her.

"No, Mari, I have no idea."

"Do you think it will be in the US?"

"I suppose so, but Mami hasn't said a word about it to me. How do you feel about it?"

"It's like an adventure. She says we will buy a lot of stuff and will have it all engraved with my name and initials. It's exciting."

"Good, I think a change will be good for you."

"Do you think I will be homesick like my first year in summer camp?"

"Why should you, Mari? It's exciting like you say, and you will meet new friends. Then when you come home to visit, everyone will roll out the red carpet for you. We'll miss you so much that we will spoil you. I think it's a winning situation for you. I think you and Mami need a break from each other, and you need a break from piano. Just think—you won't have to go to the conservatory anymore."

As usual, Olivia had the right words to make me feel better. I just wished I knew where to look up my new destination on a map.

The following day, my mother took me to buy all the essentials needed for boarding school, and Olivia wanted to come along.

"We have to buy them now and engrave everything with your name and sew your initials on your clothes. It's required for boarding school."

It was a happy day for me. I felt very important and was thrilled with my new hairbrushes, clothes brush, and bathrobe, which would all be personalized.

After a couple of days, I asked my mother.

"Mami, have you decided what school I'll be going to?"

"Yes, you'll be going to your same school. The Ursuline Mothers."

"What?" I screamed out. "I'm staying here in Havana?"

I pleaded with her not to send me there, but her mind was made up. I even tried to recruit my father, but he replied, "This is up to your mother."

Two weeks later, after all the embroidered and engraved merchandise was delivered, she packed me up and took me to school on a Sunday afternoon.

Being in a boarding school was nothing like I had imagined. The afternoons were horrendous. I would watch all my friends and my two cousins leave happily for their homes while I had to stay in that cold, gray habitat. There were only a handful of boarders, and they were different ages. My room on the third floor held a cot, a nightstand, and a dresser. The bathroom was at the end of the damp corridor. We started the day early with Mass and breakfast, and in the afternoons, Mass again. After homework, we showered, ate, prayed a Rosary, and would be in bed by 7 p.m., with lights out at 8 p.m. I had brought my black-and-white composition book, which I kept under my pillow with a pen I bought in New York with my dad. The book held my poems and my dreams. Like my diary, it was an even more precious secret. I would write until all vestige of sunlight was gone. You couldn't speak loudly or sing and dance your heart out like I would do at home all by myself in front of the mirror. The only mirror was a small one at the bathroom.

The worst part was that our house was just a few blocks away, right down the wide Avenida General Batista, and every afternoon I would go to the second-floor balcony and see the car with the chauffer and my sisters as they drove to the conservatory. They never looked up or waved. I did, until the last taillight disappeared. Then I would start to weep. I missed everyone terribly—my mom, my dad, my sisters, my room, my bed, and my stuffed lion family. But I missed Olivia the most. Why had she told me it was going to be good for me? Did she miss me?

That first weekend, the other girls went home on Sunday, but since I was new, the boarding school policy was that I wouldn't be allowed to visit home for 30 days. That was the last straw. Alone in that inhospitable place, I cried all weekend and didn't eat or leave my room. On Sunday evening Mother Superior called me in and told me I could call home.

"Hola," my mother answered.

I was overjoyed to hear her voice and started weeping again.

"Mami, please come pick me up. I can't stand this."

"No, *mijita*, you have to stay there and do what the nuns say."

"But Mami, I can't take the loneliness. I miss you so much, please come and get me," I said openly sobbing in desperation.

"The answer is no. *Punto*."

Then the words came out in desperation.

"If you don't pick me up, I will run away."

"And if you do, I will take you back."

I hadn't planned to say that, but once I did, the more I thought about running away, and the more I wanted to do it. Then I started planning it. When would it be the best time to do it? How should I do it? Regardless, I would not stay there.

Three days later, on a Wednesday afternoon after classes ended, I was bidding my cousin goodbye. Instead of going back to the school's patio, I followed her out the school door. My heart was beating fast as I quickened my pace, but Amparo the gatekeeper didn't notice. My cousin couldn't believe her eyes and must have said something, because I heard a couple of voices call out my name. Without turning back to see, I started running and ran all the way home. My mom and sisters were not home, so I went upstairs to my room and waited. That evening was bad. As usual she didn't scream, but her eyes looked wild and dark with anger. One thing she made clear was that I was going back in the morning.

Next morning, she went in to speak with Mother Superior while I sat outside her office on the wood bench. Amparo was giving me dirty looks, as I am sure she had gotten in trouble. I never knew what was said behind those doors. All I know is that my mom emerged and asked me to follow her to the car.

"Where are we going?" I asked. She didn't reply.

We were going home. She wasn't speaking to me and for weeks she wouldn't speak to me or look my way. My dinner was brought to my room. I also had to pray a Rosary every night before going to bed. Even Olivia couldn't help me. I had gone too far, and I knew it. Boarding school was never mentioned again.

3

GUSANOS

We started hearing rumors at school that the Castro militia, which had been hiding in the Sierra Maestra at the easternmost tip of Cuba, was closing in on Havana. Batista's soldiers were turning on the president, and what was left of his army was trying to prevent the revolution from reaching the capital. The bombings and assassinations were increasing, and my parents would hardly go out. They had always enjoyed going to Tropicana and Montmartre, the famed Havana nightclubs. My father would dress in a white dinner jacket, and my mom would put on her best jewelry and wrap herself in a brown mink stole. Her perfume, Nuit de Noel by Caron, filled the house as they were leaving. Cuban women would dress very elegantly during the 50s, and my mother was no exception. However, the latter part of 1958 was a scary time. There were no parties or other nightlife, and my dad would go alone to play poker.

Olivia was turning 15 and was going to have her *quince* party at the rooftop of the Hotel Havana Hilton. Because of all the bombings and attempts on the lives of Cuban government officials, her party was canceled and replaced by a Mass of gratitude followed by a breakfast. She looked beautiful at her breakfast, which included all her classmates and family. Hot chocolate was served and so was Ana Dolores Gomez's famous Encanto cake on a mirror with flowers. Olivia wore a beautiful designer dress with new Mikimoto pearls gifted to her by my mother.

"Don't worry, Olivia, you'll have a big party next year," I told her that morning on the way to Mass. She didn't answer me. She just smiled.

That summer of 1958 was the last time we went to Moss Lake Camp, but I hold dear all the beautiful moments and memories of our time there. I think of those times whenever I want to revisit my childhood. What follow are the memories I tried to erase.

My father didn't explain much and was very quiet those days. You could sense the tension he felt, especially during the end of that year. That Christmas of 1958 would be the last we'd spend in Cuba, and I remember very little of it.

On January 1, 1959, at 5 a.m., my mother woke us up after my father had been burning papers all night. "Take winter clothes," she said. "Dress warm because we are going on a trip."

Olivia helped me pick out my clothes, which included a green and black checkered pleated skirt with a matching little jacket and long coat that my mother had bought me at Bloomingdale's in New York. Half-asleep, I asked Olivia, "Are we going to New York?"

"I don't know, but you need to hurry up."

I followed her to the bathroom to brush my teeth. I saw her put some toiletries and essentials in her beige leather train case.

My mother came into the room saying, "Don't take any luggage. If we are stopped, it can't appear that we are going to travel."

Now she had my full attention, but I still didn't know what was happening. My stomach was in my throat, and I could have used a café con leche, but we rushed out without having breakfast. It was then that I noticed that the house was empty. All the servants had vanished during the night. It was still dark when we left, and my father looked serious.

We never made it to the airport because the militia had taken it over and was arresting anyone looking to flee. Batista had fled Havana, leaving the country to the Castro coup, and the militia was looking for all of Batista's officials, both military and government employees. Having nowhere to go, we made our way to the house of my favorite aunt, Elena (my father's sister). When we got out of the car, I looked back at my father as he waved goodbye. My cousins and paternal grandmother also lived in that house. The sun had risen, and my eyelids were heavy. There were four of us, and my aunt was trying to arrange where we could put our clothes and settle in. My grandmother, who was deaf, kept repeating the same question in her usual monotonous voice. "Where is everyone going to fit?" she would say unkindly. I never felt like I had a grandma. My *abuela* Maria let us know without apologies that her favorite grandchildren were those of her daughter Elena, my aunt. My cousin Pablo and her sister Elenita made up my grandmother's entire world. Whenever the ice cream man came in his cart and I was at their house, she would come out to pay for the ice cream, and I was turned away by the vendor because she would only pay for Pablo and Elenita. That hurt deeply. I daydreamed about my maternal grandmother pampering and hugging me. But that wouldn't help the current situation. Fortunately, my Aunt Elena was very loving to us. She was a widow and lived near our house. Hers was a smaller house than ours, so I knew we would have to adjust our lifestyles. "Thank God it is only for tonight," I thought.

After we left our bags in the bedroom and had some breakfast, I overheard my mother saying to my aunt, "The embassies of Chile and Peru are full, and they cannot grant him asylum. He is finding a place to go into hiding until he finds an embassy that will take him. We'll know more tomorrow."

Hiding? Asylum? I ran to Olivia to tell her what I had heard.

"They must be talking about someone else," she said. "Maybe it's the president. I'm sure that President Batista needs to leave the country right away."

My sister always knew what was going on. My parents confided in her, and she was always in the loop. I knew she was lying, because I had overheard a servant saying that Batista had already fled.

"Why do we need to leave also?" I asked. "Where is Papi?"

"We'll know more in a few days," she said. "Now you need to take off all those layers of clothing and find something to sleep in. Elenita will give us some pajamas."

I thanked God that I had Olivia. My mother looked like she was in shock, and I didn't dare to ask her anything. I went into Elenita's bedroom and found Lucia crying.

"Don't cry Luci," I said. "I think Papi is finding a place to hide."

"Hide?" she screamed out. Then she started sobbing harder.

The more I tried to comfort her, the more she cried. All I could do was hug her. We sat there crying together until we were exhausted.

That night I remember sleeping with Elenita and missing my bed and especially my pillow. My sisters slept in another bed with my mom. Then I realized that I had left my composition book under my pillow. That is where I did all my writing. I would recover it as soon as I was back home again. A few days and nights went by, and we were not allowed to step out of the house. Asking about my father's whereabouts received no response. The adults in the house had memorized the same statement: "So far, all we know is that he is safe. And that is all you need to know for now."

My grandmother complained about how long we took in the bathroom and kept asking when we would go home. Elenita was sweet to me, but at the age of 12, I really missed my bed, my room, and my stuffed animals. *The Diary of Anne Frank* had been published in English recently. My mom had bought it for us, and I had finished it in one day. Oh, how I wished I had brought the book with me. The past few days I could not help but liken my situation to hers. We did not need to tiptoe or whisper. Food was not scarce. But we had to take turns for the two bathrooms and did not go outside where the neighbors might notice us. My sisters were not allowed to call their friends or boyfriends, and no one knew where we were.

We spent our days playing board games and card games, since all the schools were closed. Pre-Castro, we had learned to play canasta from my mother. Her lady friends would come over to our house one day a week and play all afternoon while they were served coffee, tea, and pastries. I looked forward to those afternoons and the leftover petit fours. My sisters and I decided to teach Elenita to play so we could have pairs. When we needed to stretch our legs, we would go to the backyard with Pablo to fly kites. Sometimes I would sit with him and watch him build his model airplanes. TV wasn't a thing in those times, especially not during the day, so the five of us relied on our imaginations and came up with games. Whether it was precious rocks or bananas, we bought, sold, bartered, and made up new rules each day. The days went by slowly, and my mother would be gone for most of them. I learned later that she spent her time searching for an embassy that would give my father political asylum.

It was all over the news that the new regime sought members of Batista's government still in hiding. My aunt, who would go in and out of the house to shop, heard rumors that they were being executed without trial. She now saw flags of the revolution outside her own neighbors' homes. We didn't know if they had supported the revolution all along or if they now supported it out of fear, but one thing was certain—we could not trust anyone.

That night I was dozing off when I heard my mom and my *Tía* Elena talking outside. My Mom sounded upset and kept saying *Ay mi Dios*. I stepped into the living room to find that my sisters had joined the conversation.

"How can this be possible? Our own neighbors?"

They had just found out that our house had been ransacked. Ransacked? I digested the word, and a million images came to mind. Our own neighbors and Havana citizens were carried away by the romance and fervor of the "revolution of the people" and were now looting and vandalizing affluent neighborhoods and targeting the *Batistianos'* homes. My mother planned to go and salvage what she could. She wanted to leave me behind, but I pleaded and begged, so they took me along.

The next morning was January 6, the Feast of the Epiphany, or Three Kings' Day. Typically, our house would be filled with presents and all the family would get together. Today, the house was quiet, and my sisters were having breakfast with my cousins. My mother was sitting at the little telephone table with her address book, and as she picked up the receiver of the rotary phone and started dialing, I stayed out of sight to listen. She dialed two numbers, and the conversations ended fast. Neither of our two chauffeurs were willing to work for us anymore. Visibly shaken, she stood and walked chin up to the breakfast table wearing a fake smile. I followed.

We had our café con leche and buttered toast and then prepared to leave. It was a short drive, so Tía Elena would take us there. The day was cloudy, one of the few cloudy days I remember. The memories of Cuba that I hang on to and have not erased were all filled with sunshine. I held Olivia's hand and she told me not to worry. We sat in the back, and my mother sat in the front with Tía Elena.

The first thing we noticed was that the door stood open. My mother told us to stay in the car while she went to see who was in there, and a fearful Tía Elena followed her. Minutes passed and no sight of either one. Voices came from behind us. As they got closer, we could hear their words:

"Gusanos. Esbirros. Latifundistas": Worms. Henchmen. Filthy landowners.

These were the words they chose for us—the members of Batista's government. The revolution had empowered them, and they could take whatever they wanted. They called themselves the "people of Cuba." Our Father had warned us: "Make no mistake, this revolution is the beginning of communism in Cuba.

Fidel Castro, Che Guevara, and all the leaders of this revolution are communist."

Olivia told me to cover my ears, but I didn't. Lucia was already crying. The car door flew open, and it was my mom. She hurried us out of the car and tried to shield us from any harm. The screams got louder, and I was shaking. We went inside the house, and she closed the door. Nothing could have prepared me for what I saw.

Our home, our beautiful home, had been destroyed. Debris and shattered glass covered the floor. You could hardly walk across the beautiful marble floors without stepping on broken glass and porcelain. Most of the furniture either was gone or had been ripped and slashed in a rage. The air reeked of a combination of my father's liquor, his cigars, and my mother's Nuit de Noel perfume. In their frenzy, the thieves had dropped full bottles of scotch and cases of champagne while raiding our bar closet. They had also dropped bone china, the decorations, and antiques. They had even ripped out the drapery, leaving the windows bare.

The scene upstairs was even worse. The toilets and sinks had been yanked out of the bathrooms. The culprits had mistaken the fine porcelain for marble. Nothing was left in the closets or drawers. Only empty hangers and the smell of cedar wood remained in the closets. All my clothes, including underwear, my stuffed animals, my ballet shoes, all other shoes, my books, and my diary, were gone. I ran to look under my pillow where I kept my composition book. The pillow was not there, and neither was my pretty pen. My poems were gone! Who had my poems? I searched under the bed and throughout the floors and there was no trace of the composition book that held my joys and sorrows, my dreams.

Of course, none of the beautiful jewelry remained. Fortunately, the Piaget watch that my father had given Olivia for her *quince* birthday was wrapped firmly around her wrist. The violation of our privacy made me shiver. The *people* had descended on us like a pack of wolves.

I don't remember anything else after that or how we got back to my aunt's house. I remember conversations about the fact that the piano remained and that the neighbors were in on the looting. The days that followed were blurry and confusing. My father stayed at an embassy, where he had sought political asylum. He would soon leave the island, but my mother wouldn't tell us when. The militia was still posted in the corner of my aunt's house, and every time we went out, they asked about the whereabouts of our father. Fear kept us indoors.

However, there was someone who came often to check on us. I would peek through the curtains at my aunt's house and see him. His black cape, unruly hair, and long, salt-and-pepper beard were unmistakable. Like a character from the Brothers Grimm fairy tales, he roamed the streets of Havana, and children would hide behind their mothers' skirts when they saw him. He was the famed *El Caballero de Paris* (the Gentleman from Paris).

El Caballero de Paris was a troubadour straight out of Cuban folklore. He was a homeless vagabond but highly educated. He visited us frequently and knew us by name. *Las muchachitas de Lorenzo* (Lorenzo's girls) he would call us. He would wait outside our house, and my father would always stop to talk with him and give him the change in his pocket. In the afternoon, the man would often appear in front of us out of nowhere and call us by our first names. I often thought he knew our schedules at the conservatory. As he approached, he would open wide his black cape like a bat and look at us with his deep, penetrating blue eyes. From little compartments inside the cape, he would start taking out little gifts. He gave us combs, pennies, hibiscus flowers, and devotional holy cards. Then he would entertain us with tales of the Spanish war and his dreams of knighthood. He smelled of all the odors emitted by the vendors in the street, and I can't deny that I was afraid of him. But my father always said that he would never hurt us. Often, when he was present, he would allow us to sit in his lap. His smell made me cringe, but in time I lost all fear of him. My father tried to help him with housing,

24

but El Caballero refused, claiming to be a musketeer and a corsair, which confirmed that he had chosen the streets.

How he found out the address of our aunt, I will never know. We never went out to greet him, but a couple of times he caught a glimpse of me peering out. Our eyes would connect, and he would smile. Then he would turn and walk away. I have a feeling that he needed to know that we were okay.

On a gloomy day in January 1959, my uncle, a colonel in Batista's army, was tied to a pole and shot by a firing squad. I had seen him just before his death and will never forget his charismatic smile. My uncle was known to be straitlaced and honorable, a man who followed orders. Che Guevara had sworn to avenge all the attacks my uncle led against the rebels. Instead of fleeing, he remained behind, and on that infamous day in Cuban history, the rebels got their vengeance. It was a tragic day for the entire family and one that will never be forgotten. Most of the men in our family were part of Batista's government or army. I kept asking about my other uncle, a senator, but no one would tell me where he was. I was close to him and loved him dearly. Later, I heard that he, his wife, and their young son had escaped to Mexico. Our entire family had dispersed. We were running for our lives and in different directions. "What would become of us as a family?" I wondered.

Finally, the day came when my mother told us to get dressed because we were going to see our father before he left Cuba. We rode with our aunt and arrived at the Guatemalan Embassy. He and two more members of the Batista government had requested political exile. They had been in hiding at the embassy for two months and awaited arrangements for their departure to Guatemala. My father had lost so much weight, which was sad to see. While we hugged and kissed him, I took in his smell of tobacco and a different cologne. A beautiful Great Dane sat in the corner of the room staring at us. This brought me peace for some reason.

"Papi, where have you been?' I asked him. Olivia scolded me for it. My father's eyes got watery, and he couldn't say a word. This was the first time I had seen my father in such a condition.

After what seemed an eternity, he said, "I've missed you. That has been the hardest part of all."

An exchange of words between my mother and him went on for a while, but I couldn't make out what they were saying. It was time to leave, and we all cried, even my father. After we said our goodbyes, my head exploded with questions that I hadn't asked. I looked back at the sad-looking Great Dane. He never got up. Neither did my father. We were escorted out of the embassy through the same back entrance we had used to enter.

"We will see him soon," Olivia reassured me.

"Mami, why is he so thin? Where has he been? Did they hurt him?" I let it all out in one breath. I never got the answers.

It was the first time in my short existence that I felt immense fear. Riots and assemblies would appear on the news at night, and every time they showed the *people* shouting and asking for *Paredón,* which meant Firing Squad. It made me think that something dreadful would happen to my father or that something could even happen to us. I hardly slept at night. I listened for any unfamiliar noise but heard only crickets and frogs. At least my father was alive, I told myself.

We never knew what day he left the island, but a few days after our visit, a picture in the newspaper showed him leaping from a limousine holding a Guatemalan flag and stepping onto the boarding stairs without touching Cuban soil. The headlines were full of insults for "*El Esbirro Lorenzo Solano.*" I cried a lot that day. My proud and dignified father had left his island in shame.

We never went back to school or got to say goodbye to our teachers. We considered going, but my mother said that without a chauffeur or bodyguard, it wouldn't be safe. Most of my sisters' friends did not have fathers who worked for Batista. They enjoyed the novelty of seeing bearded men in olive green uniforms who had come down from the mountains to patrol the streets. Educated, prominent families were still fooled by Fidel Castro's charisma and were excited to see a "change." He even fooled President Eisenhower. Years later, once-hopeful Cubans would be running for their lives and fleeing the country in droves.

With my father gone and out of danger, my mother would allow us to play outside more. We could go for a walk but only with an adult. Castro's security knew where we were, and one or two men kept watch at the corner of the house. It didn't feel safe, so I didn't join my sisters on walks. I would say I was too tired. I didn't want to admit feeling afraid.

"We will join your father very soon," my mother would tell us. The days went slowly, and spring came and went.

I thought a lot about my father during those days. Men of Catalan descent were known for being temperamental, but he took a lighthearted approach to our girlish dramas. And I missed his goodness. He was a kind, funny, and honorable man who worked very hard to give his three daughters the best life, education, and future possible. He also gave us nannies, summer camps, conservatory, finishing schools, yacht club, and all the fineries relished by Havana's bourgeoisie. He never raised his voice or his hand to us, and, when asked to intervene in our confrontations with our mom, he would hear us out while demanding respect for our mother. He and my mom argued a lot behind closed doors, and the culprit was his poker games. They lasted all night, and he would lose a lot of money.

His life was transformed on that infamous day in 1959 when Castro launched his assault. Batista's lack of popular support, and ultimately his lack of courage, brought change swiftly and violently. It came in the form of men wearing olive uniforms and rebel beards who waved their rifles and took what they wanted at gunpoint—bank accounts, houses, vehicles, farms, sons, and daughters—all in the name of the Revolution. They declared God dead and introduced a new god named Fidel. He closed churches, kicked out priests and nuns, and banned Christmas, erasing tradition, religion, and history. The fact that he chose New Year's Day to take over Cuba ensured that he would rule over that holiday as well, for decades to come. That day, Castro destroyed my father's lifelong work and dreams. Our house, farm, and other buildings were confiscated, and my father's bank accounts were frozen. The revolution called these assets *bienes malversados*, which meant embezzled goods and properties. Money stolen from the *people*.

Friends of our family felt sorry for my father, but the reality was that all of our properties and land had belonged to my mother. Whatever salary my father had made working for the government did not compare to the amount owned by my mother's family. She was the one with all the money and real estate. But the seed had been planted in my mind. Had he stolen money from the government? From the people? My father was monumental to me and had provided for us in abundance. Was his money hard earned, or was he corrupt? I didn't have the courage to ask him. I remembered the big truck that came to our house at least once a month full of meats. The truck would pull up to the back of the house near the garage and the gate to the kitchen. A couple of men would bring in boxes of beef, chicken, and seafood that the servants loaded into a huge freezer in our kitchen.

Once I had accompanied him to his office in a government building surrounded by Batista's guards. He sat for hours in front of a stack of checks that needed his signature. He had to sign every check that covered government expenses. It seemed to take forever. Now, the man who lived abundantly with his family, was penniless and alone. He would discover a new and very different life.

4

The New Beginning

Olivia, Lucia, Elenita, and I were sprawled on the floor playing jacks, our favorite pastime. We heard my mother calling us and put the jacks away.

"You are leaving for the US next Monday," she said. "I will stay behind to try and recuperate some of the money and properties that were confiscated. I hope to win the case in court because the properties belonged to my grandfather. The attorney has already started the paperwork, and I will probably join you in a couple of months. Lucia will stay here with me. Your father has left Guatemala and has just rented a house in Miami. He will pick you up at the airport."

On Monday, July 27, 1959, Olivia and I left our beloved island, our home, and our youth. We had become women in a few months. We took with us a small suitcase packed with one skirt and two blouses each along with the few belongings not stolen by the *people* of Cuba. When they had burned the albums and diaries, we had lost the keepsakes of our childhood but not our memories. Good and bad, those memories would follow us and would shape our lives forever.

The scene at the airport was chaotic with people trying to leave. After bidding our mother goodbye, Olivia and I were taken to a small office at the rear of the airport and separated. A female rebel guard took me to an adjoining room and ordered me to take off my clothes. In another room, another guard instructed Olivia to do the same. The rebels searched us for American dollars. I trembled as the *miliciana* (militiawoman) searched me and demanded to know if I was hiding anything. Any fool could have found the money by simply following my eyes. They were fixed upon my pleated, green-and-black checkered skirt draped over a chair. The money had been sewn in the hem. I stood in my underwear in the middle of the room wearing my very first bra. I grabbed onto the back of a chair, and it was cold. The woman searched my shoes, looked inside my panties, and asked me to take off my bra. She felt my bra, squeezed it, and then sniffed it. Once I had gotten dressed, a militia man came to get me. I thought I was dead, soon to be executed. The *Paredón* chants ringing in my ears. But they let us go. Olivia and I held hands and were speechless as we walked onto the runway and climbed the stairs of the airplane that would take us away.

"Are you ok?" Olivia asked me.

"I don't know," I answered.

My hands and legs were shaking, and I felt frozen, but somehow I made it inside the plane.

As the flight of Cubana de Aviación lifted its wheels, we saw our last glimpse of Cuba. The deep green was impressive. Our royal palm trees stood erect and flawless, and little by little, they grew smaller. I strained to see them until the clouds covered them. Still in shock, I started crying. Next to me, my sister tried to hold her tears and act strong.

We shared our feelings and hugged. At least the money my mother had sent with us was safe—mine in the hem of my skirt and coat, and my sister's inside a tube of Colgate toothpaste. My mother had sold some personal belongings and furniture she had salvaged and raised almost $3,000. In 1959, that was enough for my father to get a used car in America and to buy some furniture for the house. My sister reached out for my cold hands and squeezed them.

"Don't worry, we will be back soon, Mari."

"I don't want to come back."

In Miami, my father waited at the gate for us with open arms and was surprised at what little luggage we had. He looked much older and thinner, but wore his usual, sunny smile. I hugged him tightly and started crying with joy. Ernesto, the husband of my father's cousin and a high-ranking member of the Batista military, had been in Miami for a few months and had driven my father to the airport. We got into his tiny car, and he took us to the house he had rented, which wasn't far from the airport. As we drove down West Flagler Street, we made a right turn on South West 32nd Avenue to Fourth Street. There, in the corner, was our house. He pointed at it with a worried look.

"I know it's not much, and it's very small," he explained. "But soon we will be able to get a larger one." When Ernesto let us out of the car, we kissed and hugged him goodbye and promised to see him soon.

The house was white, small, and perfectly square. Actually, I had never seen a house so small before. The whole thing was probably the size of our living room in Havana, but both Olivia and I reassured him that it was fine. We went up three steps where my father was opening the lock. Unlike the houses in Cuba, it had wooden floors just like in the cabins of our summer camp. The house consisted of two small bedrooms, one bath, a living room, a family room/dining room, and a small kitchen. There was one sleeper sofa in the living room, a table with four chairs in the family room, and a twin bed in each of the bedrooms. It felt good to have a place of our own. When I started planning where to put all my things, I stopped and looked at the little suitcase. There was almost nothing to put away. Just the few articles of clothing and a pad with a pen. I missed my Mead black and white composition book. With it went my desire to write. I doubted if I would ever write poems again. It had been seven months since I had written or made an entry in my diary. I went outside to see the trees. I was happy when I saw a small palm tree. But it was nowhere near the size of our royal palm trees that lined the main avenues in Havana. This was a coconut palm tree. Everything here was smaller. My heart shrunk.

The little kitchen was a bit dirty. I saw what seemed to be a huge cockroach running freely on the counter and screamed, which brought my father running.

"There are lots of those in Miami," he said. "They're called palmetto roaches. Hold on and I'll get the spray."

He bent down and pulled a green can and started spraying the intruders. A wave of nausea went through my body, and I asked my dad: "Do you have anything to drink here?"

My dad looked a bit nervous as he opened the small refrigerator. It held a gallon of milk, a gallon of orange juice, and another milk carton filled with water. There was a bright bulb inside, which I had never seen in a refrigerator. But I couldn't remember ever opening the door of a refrigerator. We were not allowed in the kitchen, and even if we just wanted water, a servant would bring it on a small silver tray with an embroidered linen doily.

My father opened a kitchen cabinet door, which revealed four dishes, four bowls, and four glasses. He grabbed one to pour me some water.

"Don't worry, Papi, I got it," I said, taking the glass from him.

"I'll bring pizza for dinner tonight," he said cheerfully. "I'm meeting with the manager of a pizza drive-through place this afternoon to see if I can get a job there. I'll buy a pizza for us."

Olivia and I hugged and thanked him. I couldn't help but feel sad for him. All our lives he had taken pride in procuring the best meats and seafood for his family. When guests came over, he provided enough food to feed a regiment. Everything about his life was plentiful. To my father, the most important thing after his family was abundant food and his cigars. He would sit at the head

32

of the table and beam with joy as he looked at the large trays of food being served. I loved this man who smelled of cigars and citrus cologne and who hugged us tightly and quelled our sister drama. Once a man of prosperity, he went into hiding fearing for his life and traveled to two different countries asking for exile. All this without a penny. I gave him another hug.

"We are together now, Papi. We'll be fine. Soon Mami will be here."

Olivia was more shaken than I was. Her relationship with my dad had been exceptional, and I noticed her pallor. Later that day, she sat with my father on her small bed and they had a lengthy conversation. Whatever the conversation was about I never knew, but my father came out of her room with a smile and looked relieved. She had that power, my sister Olivia. She could give you strength and make you feel better all at once. Her conversations would always end with *"dale que tu puedes,"* which meant "come on, you can do this." And that is exactly what he needed now. My sister Olivia, my hero, my mom, my best friend. I was one lucky girl.

That night we ate the pizza that my dad had brought, and it tasted delicious. We shared our experiences with him but omitted some of the airport details. We cried and laughed, and in that tiny house, we felt a glimmer of hope for the first time in seven months. My father kept saying that he couldn't have gone on without us, and that seeing us had rejuvenated him and even brought him luck. He had gotten the job at that pizza restaurant. Jobs were scarce in Miami in those days, and he didn't speak English.

"Papi, don't worry, we'll teach you English," Olivia said.

"Don't worry, *mijita*, I don't think I'll need much English. I'll be washing dishes, and we'll be back in Cuba soon."

The next morning, our father took the money we had brought and told us he was going to the bank. After that, he would go with his friend and look for a used car to buy.

Fresh out of bed, I missed my café con leche. Our dad had shown us the cereal, and Olivia served us two bowls. For the life of me I couldn't understand why anyone would start the day with cold milk and tasteless cereal. I ate my cereal dry and drank orange juice. The day was sunny and beautiful, and Olivia wanted to sit outside and get some sun. I was worried about the roaches I had seen the day before and decided I would try to clean the house. I needed the floor to be clean. Ever since I had felt the crack of glass on the floors of our looted house, I was always making sure that the floor was free of debris.

I discovered that all those hours that I was left alone in the house while my sisters went out with my mom had not been in vain. I used to follow the servants and watch their chores. The cleaning lady would first sweep and then mop. So I did just that.

From then on, a routine sank in. I would do the cleaning and cooking, and Olivia would go with my father to the laundromat.

The nights were hard. Two nights after we came, my father started working at Pizza Palace. He wouldn't come home until 2 a.m. Then 3 a.m. He would be the last one to leave, because he had to wash all the dishes and clean the kitchen.

We were alone and scared at home, so Olivia and I slept together. The small bed allowed me to be so close that I could hear her heartbeat. Soothingly, she would stroke my hair and we would sing songs of her favorite group, the Platters. Her favorite was "Only You," and mine was "My Prayer." So many nights I heard her sing "My prayer is to linger with you, at the end of the day, in a dream that's divine." Olivia was a heavy sleeper and would succumb right away. I stayed awake until I heard the pebbles of the driveway crunching as the car arrived. I listened as my father turned the keys, opened and closed the front door, and locked it. He would then open the sleeper sofa in the living room and unbuckle his pants. One leg would drop to the floor, then the next one. He would fall asleep right away, and only when I heard his snoring would I let myself fall asleep. The cigar fragrance that clung to his clothing and skin, coupled with his snoring at night, created the nearest thing to security that I knew.

Money was tight, and the refrigerator was still empty. Our meals consisted of spaghetti, tuna sandwiches, and leftovers that he would bring home from the restaurant. "Leftovers for the dog," he would tell the manager. On Sundays my father didn't work, and he would make us oven-baked chicken using a recipe that my mom had given him from my deaf *abuela*. The aroma of onions, oregano, and laurel leaves filled the house, and the meal was delicious. The weeks went by, and soon it was the end of August. School would begin in a week. I was 12 and going into seventh grade.

Olivia sat with Lorenzo in the dining table.

"Papi, I have made a decision. I am going to drop out of school and look for a job."

"Why would you do that Olivia?"

"I know that the money we brought has run out. We need things, and food is scarce. This is the best solution."

"But what will your mother say?" Lorenzo asked.

"She doesn't need to know. It would upset her, and I don't think she understands how things are here."

"Olivia, you need to finish your high school. You only have one year left to graduate."

"This is only temporary, Papi. As soon as Mami gets back, I'll go back to school and graduate."

"I can't let you do this."

"Papi, please let me do this. I want to do this for my sister. She loves going to the movie theater, and we never have any money to buy ice cream or doughnuts. She is still only 12 and needs things."

Money was scarce, so she made the sacrifice that was needed. The used car my father had bought had a hole in the floor. He hadn't noticed the hole because one of the mats covered it. Warm air would gush through the hole and would have the effect of a heater. He went back to the dealer to complain but received no help. A body shop fixed the problem for more than the cost of the car. In the meantime, we still lacked towels and sheets, pots and pans, and other housewares.

Despite struggling with money, we adapted to American life easily. We'd gone to a school run by American nuns, had attended summer camp in New York, and had read American writers like Mark Twain, Walt Whitman, and Emily Dickinson, among others. My mother had learned American ways of life from her governess and would pass them along to us. It was as if she knew we would end up living in America one day. Even though I was the first Cuban exile girl to enter Shenandoah Jr. High School, I spoke fluent English. From then on, I was no longer Maria Josefa. I was Mary Jo.

Every Sunday, Olivia brought home the newspaper and looked through the classifieds for work. She circled several jobs that interested her. They were all downtown, which was convenient, because a short walk and bus ride would get her there. Soon, she started working at Eagle Army Navy Clothing Stores folding clothes. On Saturdays, she worked at Schneer's Jewelers, also downtown. She had taken the reins of our world and had become a woman overnight. Meanwhile, our father started to wear gloves to keep his hands from bleeding; he worked nights as a dishwasher and cleaned offices during the day for a company that employed Cuban exiles (all from affluent Cuban families that had fled the island as part of the first Cuban diaspora).

On one hot Sunday, he said he would drive us to the beach. So, we made tuna sandwiches and peanut butter and jelly sandwiches. I picked a few mangos from the tree in our yard and packed them also. We went to Crandon Park, a public beach with lots of palm trees and shaded areas. I loved going to the beach with my father and enjoying a lazy afternoon with him.

"This beach is nothing like *Varadero*," my Papi would say, referring to one of the most beautiful beaches in Cuba. He had taken us there often, especially during our Holy Week break, and we had stayed at one of the hotels nearby. The water was crystal clear and the sand as white as baby powder. There my father could relax, disconnect, and be with us all day. In the mornings, he would bring a basket of tangerines, *mamoncillos* (Cuban version of lychees), and other fruit. He and my mom would lounge while we played in the water. Later, we would all have lunch in the terrace restaurant of the hotel. My father would allow his three girls to have a small glass of Cinzano wine with an egg yolk inside. Those lazy days allowed us to be family.

"Next summer," he said as we found a spot at Crandon Park beach, "we will be back, and we will go to *Varadero.*"

We said, "Yes Papi, I know we will."

After our day at the beach, we drove back in our rusted green car. Olivia and I sang, and Papi made jokes. I remember feeling happy. I felt like the luckiest person in the world.

During the week, I would come home from school and wait for Olivia to return from work. When she came home, we ate leftovers from the restaurant or homemade spaghetti. Spaghetti with tuna, spaghetti with Vienna sausages, spaghetti with ham, or just spaghetti.

"Did you finish your homework?" she'd ask.

I always said I had, even if I hadn't. Then we played Guardian Angel.

"Who was your Guardian Angel of the Day?" she would ask.

"The janitor at school. He found my pencil case. Who was yours?"

"This girl at work that helped me finish folding the clothes so I could leave on time and not miss the bus."

We believed that there were Guardian Angels everywhere and that you just had to be ready for them. If you looked closely, you would find one every day.

In our neighborhood, I became a popular babysitter. For 50 cents an hour, I babysat and vacuumed the floors.

Every day, I would walk four blocks to catch a bus for school, then transfer to another bus that dropped me off three blocks from school. The pair of shoes that I had brought from Cuba had big holes, and water would come through them when it rained.

With a little bit of money from our paychecks, our father took us downtown to buy clothes and shoes one day. Olivia brought me into a store called Lerner's on Flagler Street. The girls at school had talked about it. The mannequins on display wore wigs and pretty dresses. Although Lerner's was a lot smaller and simpler than our own *El Encanto*, it seemed to be full of nice clothes for teenagers. Olivia knew exactly what we needed and went straight to the skirt displays. She picked out two pleated skirts each. One black and one white. Two blouses each to match our skirts. That would be our wardrobe for school and many months to come. She proudly opened her wallet and paid for our clothes. I took out $8 that I had saved for personal items. The skirts were $3.99 each, so I was only going to buy one along with a top. Olivia put the money back in my wallet.

"No, Mari," she said. "Save your money for something else. I am going to pay for this."

I insisted but she wouldn't budge. A warm feeling came over me. My sister was paying for my things, and I felt overwhelmed.

"Thank you, Olivia, that's so generous of you. I don't know what to say."

"That is what Papi taught us, Mari. What is mine is also yours. There should be no distinction. I know that you are also very generous, and we will always share what we have."

Next, while our father sat waiting on a bench outside, she took me next door to Baker Shoes where she bought me two pairs of flat shoes, one black and one white. She didn't buy any for herself, although I knew she needed them.

I never forgot those words or that day. In Cuba, she had the most gorgeous wardrobe a young girl could have. Her closet was full of designer clothes and custom-made dresses. Now she went to work every day with her modest pleated skirt, although she looked as beautiful and classy as always. She never complained about her new life or about how much she missed our mother. The letters we received said that the hearing process to recuperate her real estate properties was slow. The authorities wanted her to give up and leave, but Enriqueta Mendiola was putting up a fight. I had no doubt that she would see it through to its end and would recoup what her family had left her.

Olivia continued to look out for me in other ways. She promised to take me to a special theater whenever she had the day off. The day finally came, and we went downtown to the Olympia Theater. I fell in love at first sight. The ceiling reminded me of the *Tales of the Arabian Nights*. It was painted in a voluptuous blue with dancing stars. I told her that I felt like Scheherazade and my sister laughed. The movie they were showing was *Gidget* with Sandra Dee and Jimmy Darren. Sitting there next to my sister with a bag of popcorn, I felt like the luckiest girl in the world.

After the movie ended, we went to the Five and Ten and ordered one ice cream soda to share. Our day cost only a dollar, including bus fare. On the way home, I put my head on my sister's shoulder. My mind filled with stories that I wanted to tell my mother and Lucia, whom I missed terribly. I would tell them about my new adventures at school and at babysitting jobs, where my habit of saying yes to every chore led to mishaps.

Thinking about writing to them, I realized I needed to buy a new pen. When I wrote poetry, I sometimes swore that it was my pen guiding me. I hadn't written for almost a year, and having my own pen would provide the spark I needed. I made up my mind one day to visit the drugstore near my school. The store smelled like Vick's VapoRub, candle wax, and magazines, but the place also had a warmth to it that was welcoming. After finding a lovely and inexpensive pen, I turned around and saw, of all things, a Mead composition book just like the one I once owned. I hadn't brought enough money, so I couldn't buy it. I decided I would come back after being paid for my next babysitting job.

When I brought my pen to the cash register, the cashier smiled at me.

"Are you Sandra?"

"No, I'm Mary Jo, sir."

"Oh, I've been expecting a young girl that wanted to interview for the afternoon part time job, and I thought it might be you."

"No, I just came in to look for a pen."

"Would you be interested in working here?"

That afternoon, I left Greene's Drugs with a new part-time job. I couldn't wait to get home and tell Olivia. I found her in the bedroom.

"I got a job," I told her proudly.

She turned to face me with a surprised look.

"A job? Why?" She seemed displeased. "You need to study. That comes first. Anyway, have you told Papi?"

"I mentioned it to him the other day, and he didn't respond. I went to Greene Drugs to buy a pen, and they had a job opening. It's only three afternoons a week after school for four hours and every other Saturday."

"You know that Papi is always distracted, and he probably didn't realize you meant an actual job. You know that's why I'm not going to school, so you can study hard and get good grades."

"Olivia, please, I love the smell of that place, and Mr. Greene is so nice. I promise my grades will get better."

"I don't agree that you should work," she said. "I will talk to Papi about it."

That evening, I heard them talking and my father came to the kitchen to tell me.

"You can work there, but if you get any bad grades on your report card, you will stop working."

"OK!" I was so happy. Things were tight around the house, and I knew he needed all the help he could get.

Gradually, as months passed, more and more Cubans arrived from Miami. Many arrivals included rich and educated families. The Castro regime had confiscated their businesses and had overturned their industries. Rumors that the US would sever its relationship with Cuba were surfacing, and people started fleeing Cuba in waves.

The news of my mother's victory in the Cuban courts was no surprise. She was the first Cuban citizen to get back all of her real estate. She proved in court that it had belonged to her family and that she had inherited it. The decision came with a catch: if she left the country, she would lose it all again. So, it was time for her to decide. Olivia and I had been alone for almost two years. We missed and needed our mother. We were proud of ourselves, and of the fact we were working to help our dad (none of which my mother knew about). But it had been very hard to adapt from a sheltered, affluent, and carefree life to dealing with roaches and hunger in the middle of the night. My father's parenting skills were limited, and I felt he should have insisted on Olivia attending school. But this is how Cuban fathers were—somewhat detached and unaware. Olivia and I had to go to the store for Kotex pads because he would have been too embarrassed to buy them. Also, my mother had always been on top of our grades and homework. He couldn't help me when I struggled because he himself was struggling with simple things like language. He was not adapting to this country, and he had no intention of learning English. He continued to say, "Next month we will be back in Cuba. Don't worry girls, it's just a matter of days now."

Finally, the day came: the day when my mother and Lucia finally arrived. It happened in December 1960. My mom brought with her a few things she had salvaged from the looting of our home. Some pictures, some fine linen, and embroidered towels. She was also able to ship some items that the looters had missed or left behind. Books, some Chippendale chairs from our dining room, a few Baccarat wine glasses, a couple of antique ornaments, and a set of International Silver "Joan of Arc" flatware somehow not discovered by the looters.

But why on earth would she need all these things? I asked myself. We didn't have space in our tiny house. The chairs looked completely out of place, and I had no use for stemware. I had gotten used to plastic cups. But my mother saw things differently.

"You need to be surrounded by beauty if you want to survive," she would say. "Life takes care of the ugly." Enriqueta was one of a kind, and she made her presence felt the moment she arrived in Miami.

Even though her choices confound me, now and always, I had never been so happy to see her. I kept telling her how I missed her and hugged her repeatedly. Unlike my father, she didn't look older, even after a year and a half. Instead, she looked invigorated and determined. With her, she brought hope, structure, and much-needed strength. We were a family again. But the news of my sister working was a big blow to her. She assured us that my sister would go back to school. She said maybe, only maybe, I could keep babysitting.

My sister Lucia, by contrast, was unhappy. She cried because she had a boyfriend in Cuba and he was still there. We tried to cheer her up and started asking her about her compositions. She showed us dozens of them. She had kept busy without us.

My mother's first priority was to start looking for a larger house. My father wouldn't hear of it.

"Don't bother," he said, "We won't be here much longer. Next year we will be in Cuba again."

She went shopping for new curtains and some furnishings. At night, my parents slept in the sofa bed in the living room, while we girls used the two bedrooms. Within a month, my mom had registered for classes at the University of Miami (to obtain a teaching degree) and was working as a pharmacy technician. She studied and worked day and night. She was a formidable example to us all. Her efforts dwarfed any attempt that my father made to regain his dignity.

5

HOPE

In January 1961, one month after my mother and sister arrived, the US severed diplomatic relations with Cuba.

More Cuban families arrived in droves. They included many of my sisters' friends, and they would show up at our house. People would sit on our front lawn in the evening reminiscing and dreaming of our return to Cuba. Many of them spoke about joining a brigade that was secretly preparing to overtake Castro and liberate our island from him.

Around that time, Operation Peter Pan was in full force. It was a clandestine mass exodus headed by Father Bryan Walsh of the Catholic Welfare Bureau. More than 14,000 unaccompanied Cuban minors ages 6 to 18 were brought to the US over a two-year period from 1960 to 1962. The operation was prompted by Fidel Castro's plan to terminate parental rights and send children to communist indoctrination centers and sugarcane work camps.

Two of our cousins came to the US as part of the exodus and were lodged at Camp Matecumbe in South Florida. We would pick them up on Sundays, until their parents and sisters came to Miami. Then they all stayed in our house for a while until they found jobs and rented a place. Other children weren't so lucky and stayed at the camps until the US government found foster homes for them.

Our house was a gathering place for the young, misplaced exiles. They came to talk and share news. Some of the boys came on motorcycles, others walked or rode a bus, and a few drove their parents' old cars there. They were the interrupted generation. They had lost their innocence through multiple tragedies and acts of violence. Some of the young men made rash decisions that would later affect the rest of their lives. My sister was popular among them and a great host. People brought things—fruit from their backyards or french fries from McDonald's—and put them in a basket to share. Everyone took turns until the food disappeared.

We all learned to get by on less. Before my mom and Lucia arrived in Miami, Olivia and I would go grocery shopping at Grand Union, where we could get S&H green stamps. We sat and licked stamps and glued them to a booklet. If you filled the booklet, you could exchange it for housewares and other premiums. I will never forget the day that Olivia announced, "Finally! We have enough for a toaster."

My father took us to the S&H redemption center where we brought our booklet. The attendant gave Olivia a box. We waited till we got to the car to open it.

"It's red!" she said wide eyed. "No more toast burning in the oven."

That morning, we used it for the first time. I swear toast had never tasted so good.

We had learned to improvise and adapt to Miami's culture and ethos. Schools here had hundreds of students, and young people came home to empty houses. Parents worked all day and on the weekends. Instead of going to the club, the beach, or Sunday tea dances, they mowed their lawns, cleaned their houses, and washed their clothes. Life was built around work and sacrifice. Olivia and I had begun to adapt to this life. Meanwhile, her friends shared food on our lawn, gazed at the stars, and waited for a plan.

My mother, who hadn't cooked a day in her life, began to compile family recipes and jot them down in a brown notebook. Then she started to cook for us. The first few days she burned rice and left chicken raw, but little by little she got the gist of it and started serving us good, balanced meals. My sisters, who had been learning to drive, asked my father to take them to their driver's license tests. They both passed, and my mom, who didn't drive, announced that they needed a car. On her day off, we went to look for cars at the Joseph Abraham Ford dealership on Southwest Eighth Street. My father dropped us off there because he had to go to work at the restaurant. We entered the showroom through wide glass doors and saw the shiny, waxed cars on display. We had never been to a dealership because our family had used government cars in Cuba. I was dazzled.

The salesman asked Olivia and Lucia what kind of car we were looking for. While they talked, I got inside different cars and daydreamed about having my own. I turned steering wheels and opened glove compartments, but only until my mother called me. We all sat in a small office for what seemed like a lifetime. The salesman kept leaving to talk to his manager because my mom was negotiating like a pro. Finally, both sides agreed on a price for the white four-door Ford Falcon with a gray interior. The tag application process and car prep took another couple of hours, and the sun was almost setting by the time we left, but we eventually started the ride home. Lucia had won the toss, and Olivia and I sat in the back seat.

From then on, my sisters drove my mother to work and themselves to school. My school was out of their way, so I happily continued my adventures on the Tigertail bus on 32nd Avenue. Our quality of life was improving because our mom had taken the reins. I was no longer incorrigible. I was grateful to this country for opening its doors to us and even more grateful for my mom's brave leadership.

During this period, President Eisenhower ordered the CIA to train a brigade of more than 1,400 paramilitaries—made up of Cuban exiles—for an invasion of Cuba. The CIA recruited from active exile groups in Miami, and many were my sisters' friends. They were to leave for a camp in Guatemala. Once there, they received training in weapons, infantry tactics, land navigation, amphibious assault tactics, team guerrilla operations, and paratrooping. Their instructors were from the Army Special Forces, Air Force, Air National Guard, and the CIA. Thirty-nine of the recruits were pilots who had flown in Cuba's military or as commercial pilots. Fathers and their sons of age had left for this clandestine camp in complete secrecy. Even their families did not know their whereabouts for a year. The only explanation they gave is that they were enlisting in the army. In reality, the CIA was planning a full-scale invasion.

In the early morning hours of April 17, 1961, under the new presidency of John F. Kennedy, the full-scale Bay of Pigs invasion, intended to be "both clandestine and successful" turned out to be "too large to be clandestine and too small to be successful." The 2506 Brigade of more than 1,400 men arrived by sea at Playa Giron and stormed the island's southern shore, known as the Bay of Pigs. But Castro was ready for the "secret" operation. The men were outnumbered and ambushed. They were killed or taken prisoner. Aerial support from the US military never came. President Kennedy, who had inherited Eisenhower's plan, was not willing to intervene, which doomed the invasion. When President Kennedy applied the brakes and backed off, he left Cuba to the communists.

My father was shattered. He had been waiting over two years for this moment. All the Cuban exiles were devastated. They had known the invasion would take place, but the date was a secret. That Monday, no one went to work, and every Cuban family in Miami was glued to the TV and radio. For two days the whereabouts of the men were unknown. Some of them had drowned attempting to reach a US destroyer near shore that was under fire and was forced to retreat. Other men ran to the hills to hide. It took days to account for everyone. Seventy-five percent ended up in Cuban jails, while the others died in battle.

**

After this debacle, Olivia decided to go visit her friend Ana Garcia. Her father had participated in the invasion, and his whereabouts remained unknown. Olivia parked her car in the pebble driveway of Ana's house. Nervously she pressed the handles of her small purse and headed to the door. She knew how sad everyone would be and didn't quite know what to say, but she felt she needed to be there. Ana's mother greeted Olivia at the door with a smile and asked how Lorenzo and Enriqueta were doing, which relieved my sister. Friends and family were there. Olivia said hello to everyone and sat with the group of young people that tried to comfort Ana. Olivia gave Ana a kiss and sat next to her. The group was playing a fortune-telling game to pass the time, so she joined them. After a while, the doorbell rang, and Ana's mom went to the door. As soon as Antonio "Tony" Del Rio walked into the room with two other young men, Olivia recognized him as the "naughty boy" who had been kicked out of the Miramar Yacht Club in Havana for peeping under the stalls in the ladies' room. He was drop-dead gorgeous, and she had always been attracted to him. The three young men had been on one of the ships at the time of the invasion. Their mission was to secure strategic positions in the island after taking possession on the beach, but since the invasion had failed, they never got off their ship. The boys joined the others in the game, and Olivia felt Tony's eyes on her. She learned from their conversations that Tony had just broken up with his girlfriend. Her heart was beating so fast that she thought everyone could hear it. All the girls in Havana liked Tony. She thought, *Just keep your head down, Olivia, and don't look straight into his eyes or he will notice.* The night went by too fast as Tony and Olivia gave each other quick glances. Each avoided staring at the other. Soon it was past 10 p.m. Enriqueta, always mindful of proper etiquette, had taught her daughters not to overextend their visits into the night. Olivia got up, hugged Ana goodbye and promised to keep in touch, and then went to thank Ana's sleepy mom.

"Thank you for coming, Olivia," Ana's mom said. "Please say hello to your parents for me."

"Of course," Olivia said. "They send their regards, and my mom said to tell you that she is praying for your husband to come back safe. Thank you for your hospitality."

Olivia then turned and gave a collective wave to the boys. She barely stopped at Tony's staring eyes. The girls followed her to the door and said their goodbyes. She got into her car and drove home.

That night, she laid in her bed with her eyes wide open while her mind raced. She moved her head to avoid the glare from the stubborn streetlight that shone through her window. *Could this be fate or just a coincidence? Tony had just arrived in Miami and he was single! He was also perfect.* She thought of the dances and the tea-dance parties on Sundays at the club where she had seen Tony cheek to cheek with his girlfriend. She always thought Tony and his girlfriend made a beautiful couple. She was a brunette with hazel eyes and adorable dimples, and he was the most handsome boy in Havana. Olivia and Tony had never shared a word, but their eyes had met casually at the club. Now she felt lonely and so ready to love and be loved by someone, but she was always exhausted when she came home from work. On weekends, she went to the movies downtown with Mari or to the beach, where she would lie under the shade of the palm trees at Crandon Park and pass out. She didn't think the interaction with Tony would go any further than a couple of glances. Every girl she knew would give anything to date him, and she didn't have the energy to flirt. She felt so old sometimes and wondered if it showed. Her favorite song by the Platters started playing in her head, and her eyelids became heavy. *"Only you can make this world seem right, only you can make the darkness bright."* Soon she rolled to her side avoiding the streetlight and fell asleep dancing in Tony's arms. She wasn't lonely anymore.

The next morning, she woke up to Lucia singing one of Debussy's compositions. Lucia had finished high school while in Havana. She was very bright and studious, so she homeschooled and passed all the required final exams before arriving in Miami. Once she got to Miami, our mother had her apply to various universities for music scholarships. This was humiliating for Olivia since she was one year older than Lucia but still needed to finish high school.

I was a member of the choir at school, and one day I tried out for an operetta that would be performed at the end of the school year. I thought I had no hope of getting picked for the cast, but to my surprise, I got the lead! As the performance got closer, I received instructions on what to wear, and I panicked. Other than a few extra blouses that Lucia had made for me, I was still wearing my pleated white and black skirts. Lucia loved to sew, and our neighbor, Shirley Scheinn, had a sewing machine. Shirley would let Lucia use her sewing machine, and I would bake cookies or make pineapple-upside-down cake for Shirley. Lucia called it bartering. So when my wardrobe crisis came, I baked a two-layer cake for Shirley, and Lucia used the sewing machine to make a nice Spanish full skirt and an off-the-shoulder blouse. The character I played, Margot, was from the south of Spain. Lucia found the right material downtown and made me the most beautiful Spanish clothes you could imagine.

Shirley had been a godsend to our family from the beginning. She lived two doors away, and from the first day she brought over her young son and baby daughter to introduce herself, I loved her. She was sincere and caring. Right away, I started babysitting for her, and she would find any excuse for me to come over and earn extra money. She even wanted to pay me to teach her how to dance the cha-cha. I learned about Jewish traditions at her house. During Passover, I helped her clean the pots and pans and bring down new dishes in preparation for the seder, and she gave us all her bread and anything containing yeast. She also taught me how to make matzo ball soup and cheese blintzes with warm raspberry sauce. This quiet, simple, and generous woman really cared about me. She would listen to my plans and encourage me to keep on writing. She was always alone with her two children, and, without realizing it, I would pass by her house almost every day to check on them. She had become family to me. From her, I learned about the solemn Jewish rituals and their history. I grew to love and respect the Jewish religion and sense of family legacy. In many ways their culture was like ours—rich in tradition.

The afternoon Lucia sewed my skirt for the show, the postman delivered the mail with a letter for her. I was home from school and saw it. Right away I knew how important it was. She had been accepted by the Juilliard School in New York and had been offered a scholarship. This was the best news we'd received in more than two years. When my mother got home, she made a special dinner to celebrate. Nothing could have pleased her more than one of her daughters becoming a real musician. Lucia was gifted and was now on her way to a career in music.

It felt like everything was coming together, including our family. I sat outside in the yard in the shell-shaped metal lawn chair with my composition book and watched how the evening breeze played with the few items of clothing on the clothesline. A bright bulb above the rear door allowed me to see when the sun was setting. Everything was in harmony at this hour. Everyone was safe inside their homes. The tranquility of the night allowed me to think clearly and empty my mind. I could hear music everywhere. Vivaldi would play in the wind and complete the moment. Classical music had always centered and inspired me. I had missed the opportunity to become a pianist but could still express myself through poetry:

If days were our palace, where we find our refuge
the fields were our slumber
the children our prayers,
the laughter and music our language,
then we could survive....

Sadness would sometimes creep up on me. I regretted being difficult early in life and wished I could turn back time and change my ways. Sometimes I just sat and cried about different things. I cried for my father, who worked so hard his fingers bled. His arthritis was so painful that I learned to warm up some wax so he could dip his fingers and find some relief. For Olivia, who always sacrificed herself. She had given up piano and had missed an entire school year. She would stay up waiting for me to get home from my babysitting and cleaning jobs. For sweet Lucia who tried so hard in everything she did and had only her music to express herself. For my lost childhood and aimless life. Adding to my sadness and worry was my mom. This woman had overcome so many obstacles and was trying to put the pieces together in a new and more difficult life. "Soon, we will have saved enough to put a down payment in a house," she would say. We had started giving the money we made to her instead of my father. The more she tried to bring stability to our lives, the deeper my dad sank into despair. He just wanted to go back to Cuba and refused to go to the English classes my mother had found for him. I hurt for the young men of the invasion who had lost their lives or were in prison. Sometimes I returned to my bed without writing a word, and sometimes I would write until late. No one would notice. Everyone was tired and asleep. The night was mine alone.

***

Olivia sat at the telephone table with the address book on her lap and dialed Ana's number.

"Hello, Mrs. Garcia, this is Olivia. How are you?"

She heard someone sobbing at the other end and then Ana came on.

"Hello, Olivia," Ana was also sobbing, "now is not a good time, can you call later? They found my father, and he is dead." She screamed out and hung up the phone.

The next day, it was all over the news. His body was pulled from the water just like those of many other Cuban soldiers who had tried to swim out to the US destroyer. Their bodies were riddled with bullets. Olivia decided to wait until the next day to visit Ana. The scene was heartbreaking. Ana was an only child, and she and her mother cuddled together sobbing and praying. The house was full of family and friends, and everyone was crying. Olivia started crying too.

"I'm sorry, Ana," she kept repeating. "I'm so sorry."

Olivia couldn't imagine how she could live if something happened to her own father. Driving back home, she thanked God that her Papi was safe and vowed to visit Ana often.

That day when she got home, Olivia waited for our father to come home from work and made him a warm café con leche and Cuban toast. They sat and spoke about the death of the Bay of Pigs soldiers and hugged each other tight before going to bed.

Olivia visited Ana again a few days later, but there was no sign of Tony. Finally, the following week, she saw Tony again. They sat and talked together for a while, but she was late for work and left quickly. Her head was spinning, and she felt elated as she drove downtown. She parked her car in the municipal parking lot and walked one block to the Army and Navy store where she punched in just a minute before her shift started. She started taking clothes out of the boxes and separating them, but she couldn't stop thinking about Tony.

Ana and her family were close friends of Tony del Rio and his family. She told Olivia what she knew about him. He came from a wealthy Havana family that owned sugar refineries. He was a bright but mischievous young man who had gone to a Jesuit school and struggled with conduct, which kept him from getting good grades. The oldest of two brothers, he had learned to speak out for his rights and would often get into fights. Gifted, and with abundant good looks, he was popular with the girls. He and his brother had been among the first youngsters to arrive in Miami through Operation Peter Pan and were relocated to separate homes in Connecticut. Fortunately, his mother came to the US six months later, and the family went back to Miami to join her. His father remained behind in Cuba because he had been arrested for carrying and hiding weapons. His mother had smuggled money out of Cuba in the wheels of a car that came to the US via ferry boat. The family's financial situation was more secure than that of most exiles, so Tony did not have to work. However, Tony had refused to finish his high school and instead chose to join the CIA's ill-fated effort to invade Cuba. His demeanor was quiet and observant, which made him mysterious. That fascinated Olivia.

After Olivia left Ana's that night, Tony said his goodbyes and got into his Ford Fairlane Galaxie convertible with the retractable hard top. He thought about how attractive she was and also about how bad the timing was. He had just returned from a meeting with his CIA handler and a debriefing on their new operation. After the failure at the Bay of Pigs, he had decided to stay with the CIA for good. His father was jailed in Cuba, and Tony wouldn't stop until he could get him out. The CIA had put together an operation called *Perro Negro* (Black Dog) to infiltrate the island, spy on the activities of the Communist occupiers, and recruit both *campesinos* (Cuban farmers also known as *guajiros*) and collaborators on the island to attempt another invasion. The CIA had to smuggle weapons into the island and hide them in strategic locations. But the first phase of the Black Dog mission would involve recruiting young Cuban refugees eager to liberate their home country.

As a key recruiter, Tony knew that some difficult months lie ahead. He thought of this when he first saw Olivia at Ana's house. He remembered her right away from the country clubs of Havana. Her classic beauty and serenity reminded him of Grace Kelly. He thought Olivia was one of the prettiest girls he had ever seen. Her long hair was light brown and glowed in the sun. Her elegance turned heads when she walked. He had never gathered up enough courage to approach her, but now they had finally met. He knew that all the boys liked her, so he planned to act quickly before they did. The only challenge was his job with the CIA. He had been warned that he would have to travel often and must never tell anyone, not even his mother or brother, about his work or where he was going. And now, he did not know how to explain his comings and goings to Olivia. He had to use his imagination.

***

It was Friday, payday, and Olivia parked her car behind Greene's Drugs and waited for me to come out from work. From there, we would go to McDonald's. I felt on top of the world with that envelope in my hand. With all the uncertainties around us, simple times like these were refreshing.

Mr. Greene would give me my envelope after the last shift on Friday. I looked inside at all the money I earned—$12 and change. I usually kept $1, sometimes $2 if we planned to go to the movies that weekend. Olivia never knew how excited I felt when I got into the car with her. Fridays had become my favorite day of the week. We drove to McDonald's as usual and ordered cheeseburgers and fries.

"So, tell me, Olivia," I asked as she picked at the fries, "what did Tony say when you saw him the other day?"

"He wants to take me with his friends to a dance in Miami Beach next weekend. He sat next to me as soon as he came in and started talking. It's *el baile de los viejos* next Saturday."

She was referring to the dance sponsored by the City of Miami Beach. It was held on South Beach's Fifth Street bridge and had become highly popular. Because Miami Beach was a place where seniors retired, the event was called "Dance of the Seniors," but the young outnumbered the old.

Tony and Olivia had made plans to attend.

"Do you think he is the one?" I asked

"Mari, I need to get to know him better, but I've always liked him. Looks aren't everything, you know."

"Yes, but it helps. I couldn't kiss an ugly guy."

54

We both laughed. I felt like her confidante and wouldn't trade those Friday evenings for anything in the world.

The week passed slowly. Finally, Saturday arrived and Olivia stood in front of the mirror in her room. She wore a light-yellow, cotton pique dress. She put on her pearl earrings and a small pearl necklace and applied lipstick as a final touch. "A woman shouldn't go out without earrings, lipstick, and a smile," Enriqueta would always say.

"I need to get some decent perfume next week when I get paid," Olivia said as she sprayed some Jean Naté behind her ears and on her wrists.

I caught a glimpse of Tony as they said goodbye to my mom at the door. He was taller and more handsome than I had imagined him. I peered through the blinds and watched them join the other friends in his car. That was the beginning of the story of Tony and Olivia. They looked so happy that early June night. No one could foresee what lay ahead.

It was an exciting summer. Lucia was getting ready to leave for Juilliard. My mom bought her a used sewing machine, and Lucia sewed away. Lucia was incredibly talented and soon made herself a new wardrobe from scraps of material given to her by the lady at Diamond's store, where Lucia worked.

Olivia was also working and getting ready to start school again. She was also falling in love. Tony would come around at night and sit and hold hands with her in the shell-shaped metal chairs.

My mom attended the University of Miami that summer in pursuit of her teaching degree. She studied a lot and also worked at the pharmacy. I kept busy with my babysitting and had picked up more hours at Greene Drugs. My poor father was still cleaning offices and washing dishes. I can't imagine how he made it through every day. In Cuba, he used to leave for work every morning in his white linen suit and straw hat looking like Humphrey Bogart. Everybody knew him and would wave or approach him with respect. Now I saw a man walking out of the house with his head down dressed in a pair of worn-out brown pants and a T-shirt. The only thing that kept him going was the certainty that before the year was over, he would be back in Cuba. Only that thought brought a spark to his eyes.

6

THE LIE

My mother always found ways to involve us in everything cultural and musical. Olivia was an excellent ballerina and an accomplished pianist. Her ballet performances in *Swan Lake* and *The Nutcracker* in Havana had been superb. When Castro marched into Havana, we lost our music and dance. There was no piano in Tía Elena's house, and our ballet shoes and uniforms were gone. For more than two years, we hadn't practiced anything that involved either discipline. One day, my mom took Olivia to the Miami Conservatory to meet with Thomas Armour of Ballet Russe. The goal was to obtain some kind of scholarship or financial assistance. When they both came back home, Olivia expressed her objection: "Mami, how can I audition for them next week? I haven't practiced, held a barre, or danced in over two years!"

"Don't worry, Olivia. I already explained to him the situation, and he seems like a very nice man."

"Nice has nothing to do with it, Mami. Did you see those dancers? They were flying across the stage like birds! I can't do a *grand jeté* like that anymore. I would need months to practice."

"We have nothing to lose," Mami said. "It's a great opportunity for you. Or would you rather resume with your piano instead?"

"I haven't played a piano for over two years, but yes, it's more likely that if I played now, I wouldn't make a fool out of myself. I'm not physically in shape for a ballet audition."

"OK, I will see where there's a piano conservatory in the city. You are very talented Olivia, and you need to resume your piano or ballet."

"How can I have private piano lessons when my father is washing dishes, and we barely have enough to eat?"

"I'm starting my new teaching job in August, and things are going to change. You are going to be able to resume your piano or ballet, we are going to buy a larger house, and we are going to have medical insurance. In that order."

"Mami, sometimes I think that you still believe that we are in Cuba," Olivia said. "I will not let you spend one penny on ballet or piano while my father cleans floors and washes dishes. Or my sister has to hold a job at the age of 14. This is our reality."

I felt they were both right, and I just listened in frustration. I dreamed of seeing my sister dancing or playing piano again, but our world had transformed. Our privileged life in Cuba seemed like a totally different world right now. Here to stay was a new life full of struggles but greater purpose. I felt useful to my family, proud of myself, and closer to God. I would pray more fervently than ever, and He would listen. Sometimes I would leave Him alone because my needs and wants were getting out of hand. My cousin, Father Vicente, would always tell me to "put things in God's hands, and He will bear our weight on his shoulders." I was really loading God up lately, and all, in all I can say that I felt He was taking care of us. Every morning when I left the house, the first thing I would do is look up to the sky, smile, and thank Him. Thank you is the best prayer.

Lucia sat next to me in my bed that night. She said, "You know that you are a good pianist and a great dancer, don't you?"

"You and Olivia are the good ones."

"You don't fool me," she said. "You just don't want to put in the work, but I have seen you at the piano and your form en pointe.

You could be a great pianist or ballerina if you stopped being so rebellious."

"Thank you for saying that, Luci. It means a lot."

"I'm only saying that because it's true. You are as talented as we are."

I went outside to my shell-shaped chair to look at the stars. Everything looked prettier at night. My dreams were more vivid, and my future seemed brighter at night. Van Gogh said that the night was more richly colored than the day. He was right. Lucia had reminded me that my chance had passed. She was right, too. I just wished that Olivia could continue.

Enriqueta would find a way. I noted this in my black-and-white composition book.

On a Sunday in mid-August, we took Lucia to the airport to catch a flight to New York. My mom couldn't accompany her because we didn't have enough money for two tickets, so Lucia went alone. She looked so scared that I started crying.

"Why are you crying, Mari?" my mother asked. "This is a very happy occasion for the entire family. Lucia is going to fulfill her dream of becoming a composer and conductor."

I could tell Olivia was holding back tears as she clung to my father's arm.

My mom never cried in front of us. I used to hear her at night at Aunt Helen's house in Cuba or sometimes in her room after a fight with my father. Once, she wiped something from her eye that I know was a tear, but she said it was a twig or an eyelash. I wondered if she cried mostly out of anger, sadness, or humiliation. Did she cringe, or did she just let it flow? Did she dry her tears right away or bury her head in her pillow and sob? I would look for signs so that I could run to her and hug her. How I wished we could have seen her vulnerability. But she never allowed it. She had to keep her composure.

"Luci, make sure to call us when you get there," my dad said. "Don't talk to strangers in New York. The city has bad areas, so stay away from them." He hugged her goodbye.

My parents stayed behind while Olivia and I walked Lucia to the boarding gate. When we all hugged, there wasn't a dry eye. Lucia looked thin, pale, and scared. It was a big step for her; she was only 17.

She walked out to the tarmac, climbed the stairs to the airplane, and waved back at us. Someone from Juilliard was going to meet her and set her up in the dorms. I spoke with God again and asked Him for another favor. I'm sure He heard me.

Back in the car, there was a lot of sniffling, and suddenly my father said, "Let's go to Toby's Cafeteria and have lunch. I think it would do us good and cheer us up."

My father, and almost every Cuban person I know, was convinced that everything could be cured with food. He would say, "Once you eat a nice juicy steak, you'll feel better." Or "Have some dessert. It will put you in a good mood." We couldn't afford steaks anymore, but apple pie à la mode had been doing the trick for me lately.

We arrived at Toby's Cafeteria 20 minutes later. Olivia and I felt better. Seldom did we go out to eat, and when we did, it was for a special occasion. My dad's favorite was Sweden House, an all-you-can-eat buffet, but I preferred Toby's and their turkey with stuffing, mashed potatoes, and green beans. I often craved turkey with stuffing after our second Thanksgiving meal in the US. Alice, my mother's governess, hosted us. She and her husband, a former judge, were retired and now lived in Miami. Alice and my mother had kept in touch throughout the years, and she invited us to their cozy home in Miami Springs for Thanksgiving. It was a magical evening that featured delicious, traditional Thanksgiving dishes, which were new to us.

At Toby's, my mouth was watering when I got into line with my tray. Olivia handed me a place setting. Her favorite was the fried shrimp, and my parents liked the roast beef. We rolled the plastic cafeteria trays through the stations picking out our favorites and making sure to keep it to a minimum. Salads and side dishes would make the bill too expensive.

We found a booth and let the food do its magic. What had started as a sad day became a happy one. We talked and made jokes while we ate. My father was in good spirits. He had tried hard to make us laugh and had succeeded. Olivia and I hugged and thanked him. Then it was time to go home because he had to go to work.

Olivia was quiet on the way home. She sat in the front with our father. She was worried about Tony. He had started selling the *Encyclopedia Americana*, and his job consisted of traveling to universities and selling to students. Lately, he kept the entire 30-volume set in the back of his car. It was one thing to be a traveling salesman, but Olivia didn't understand why he couldn't call home while he traveled. This time, she hadn't heard from him in more than a week. She never knew that being in love could hurt so much and cause so much distress.

Whenever Tony was in town, they would spend as much time together as they could, only to be separated by another trip. She did, however, look forward to going back to school in a few weeks and had given notice at the Army and Navy store. She would still work at Schneer's Jewelry, but only on weekends. My mother had made clear to us that school would be our priority, and she did not tolerate bad grades.

The week went by fast. On Friday, Olivia drove to school to pick up the textbooks I would be using that year. They would have been too heavy to carry on the bus. When she brought them home, I looked at the names of the students who had used them before me. I would soon mark my place in each book's history.

Olivia sat down with me. "Let's cover your books." She always made time to help prepare for the big day.

We took out the brown grocery paper bags that we had kept from our shopping and started cutting and folding corners to fit the books. Olivia was a master at this, and in the time it took me to do one, she had finished all the rest. One by one, I wrote my name in them and said a silent prayer. Math was my worst subject, but I loved English and history. I made my name bigger in those books.

"Hurry up, it's almost 4:30," Olivia said. "Let's go to Krispy Kreme."

Every afternoon at around 4:30 p.m., the trays of warm, freshly made doughnuts were taken off the rollers and placed in display cases at Krispy Kreme, which was only six blocks from our house. There was nothing like a warm doughnut, and Olivia always seemed to pick the right day for a treat.

There were no customers when we arrived, and Joe greeted us with a big smile. "Hello ladies. Just in time for a nice, warm glazed donut. Haven't seen you in a while."

"It's been a busy summer," said Olivia, "but we've missed coming."

"And my sister has a boyfriend," I added, "so she is even busier now."

"You're too much," Olivia said as she patted my head.

We sat in the silver stools with the red pads, Joe brought us big glasses of water with perfectly shaped ice cubes. We started sipping and savoring our delicious doughnuts. I felt lucky to have such a great sister, not to mention a Krispy Kreme doughnut shop only a short walk from home. My papi was right. Something sweet always made you happier.

We wiped our mouths, and each got out a dime to pay. Joe would hand us back two pennies each, which we always left as tip.

At home, there was some commotion. Mami had just learned that our Tía Elena, with our cousins Elenita and Pablo, would be leaving Cuba soon. Pablo was about to turn 18 and would have to join the communist army if they were to stay. They planned to catch a flight out of Havana and then another one to Miami. As political exiles, they would get their alien number and later their residency. I was thrilled knowing that I would see my cousins again. My mother said they would stay with us for a while until they found jobs. They were the first ones to come and stay with us. For the next couple of years, the rest of the family followed until all the Solanos and Mendiolas were out of Cuba.

That week, Tony returned from one of his work trips and came to visit Olivia. She watched him get out of his car and held her breath. He looked so handsome in his jeans and polo shirt. She couldn't wait to hug him.

Up close, he looked taller and thinner than before. She put her arms around his neck and buried her face on his chest. They walked to the yard and sat underneath the mango tree. Their voices could be heard through the kitchen window.

"I've missed you so much, Tony! I didn't hear from you for so long that I was worried sick. How are you? Where have you been? Why haven't you called me?" She had let it all out in one breath.

"Olivia, you can't put this pressure on me," he said. "I travel with my boss, and he can't have all this nonsense."

Olivia stepped back to look at him.

"What do you mean? There are phones in the hotel rooms, and you haven't even called me. Haven't you missed me?"

"Of course, I missed you. But it's not possible to call because my boss is with me. We already spoke about this. I can't be calling my girlfriend."

"If you missed me and loved me like you say, you would find a way to call me. At least once during a 10-day trip. And anyway, why don't you sell to students here in Miami?"

"They have other salesmen here," he said. "I've been assigned to other universities."

"But Tony, this isn't normal," she said. "You can find a phone booth then and call me. It's too many days. What does your mom say about this?"

"She doesn't worry. She knows I'm working."

Olivia felt like a fool. *Was she wrong to ask this of him?* She was confused and began to tear up.

"Please don't get upset, Tony. I just feel nervous about these trips, and I miss you a lot."

My father, who was sitting in the living room watching the news, called out to me: "Are they still talking?"

"I think so, Papi."

"Your mother made *carne con papa,*" he said. It was the Cuban version of beef stew. "I'm late for work and your mom is napping, but I don't know if everything is OK. It sounds like they're having a fight."

"Don't worry Papi, I'm here. You can go to work."

"I'll try to bring home some pizza later."

I watched my father as he went to the bedroom to change into his work clothes. He came out dressed in white and holding his apron. We had been in Miami for a little over two years, and his hair had grayed considerably. The bags under his eyes were permanent now, and the glow had gone from his eyes. He looked so tired that I wished he could have gone back to sleep. We kissed, and he left.

I walked back to the kitchen and saw the usual pile of dishes in the sink. My mom was also always tired. She worked, went to school, and did homework. The fact that she also cooked for us was incredible and very much appreciated, but I have never seen someone use so many pots, drainers, spoons, and skillets. Every time she cooked it was as if a tornado had hit the kitchen, but the food was delicious. She relied on her brown, leather-bound notebook full of recipes from her mother-in-law, a fabulous cook. My mean grandmother used to make delicacies like baked coconut macaroons, nougats, creamy rice pudding, and *torticas de morón*. She always hid her treats from us, so I only got to taste a few. Her main dishes were also formidable. My favorite was her *arroz con pollo*, which my mother learned to perfect.

In her early attempts at cooking, my mom burned the chicken, splashed tomato sauce all over the stove, left milk boiling until it spilled, and cut herself chopping onions. But she didn't give up. Within a few months, she was preparing delicious meals large enough to give us leftovers for days. Her arms were full of burns, and she had lost most of her eyebrows when a skillet of oil caught fire in front of her. Gone were the manicured nails and her beloved masseuse. A tremendous work ethic now defined her. She was never absent or late for her shifts. Not once did I hear her complain, nor did she feel sorry for any of us when we complained.

She realized we were in the US to stay and would often make the point to my father, who insisted we would be in Cuba by the end of the year. She wanted to buy a house and establish roots. He was opposed. I was afraid to go back to Cuba and secretly hoped that we would stay in Miami.

Suddenly, I heard the front door slam and saw Olivia go straight to her room, and I followed her. She had been crying but was composed.

"What's wrong, Olivia?" I asked.

"I'm exhausted and don't want to talk about it, but I know he's lying about something."

"What do you mean lying?"

"Just that. He's lying. Something is not right with those trips, and I'm going to find out about it."

"Don't worry too much, Olivia, he will probably get bored of that job. It's a salesman job. Nothing exciting." I was trying to cheer her up. "Do you want to eat the *carne con papa* that Mami made?"

"I'm not hungry. I'm going to take a shower and go to bed."

I sat down to eat by myself. The sound of the ceiling fan and the crickets outside kept me company and created a lulling rhythm that I liked. I finished the dishes and started on homework.

My worst subject was math, and I had a test the next day. My father was a whiz at numbers, but he was never around. Alan, one of the boys in school, had offered to help me, but I was too embarrassed to accept. My mother had gone to bed after cooking, and Olivia was upset. I tried to figure out the new algebra problems and stayed up for as long as my eyes could remain open, which wasn't long. I kept thinking of my math grade. It was my only D. I got into my bed close to midnight. The words of my favorite heroine, Scarlett O'Hara, came to mind: *I'll think about it tomorrow.*

7

The Truth

Olivia lay in her bed with her eyes fixed to the ceiling. The glow of the streetlight made her get out of bed and close the blinds. She saw a beautiful half-moon in the sky on this clear August night, but she felt a storm brewing within her. *How can I be falling in love with a man who disappears for weeks at a time? It doesn't seem fair that he expects me to accept this. I know he likes me, but there is something wrong with this job he has. God, please help me make him see this.* Tears rolled down her cheeks, and she did nothing to stop them. She felt the pressure on her chest to the point she could hardly breathe. *I'm so tired, God. I feel miserable, and I miss my life in Cuba, my piano, and my school. I feel so selfish worrying about Tony when I can't even help my family. Please help us. Help my father get a different job so his hands can heal.* She cried endlessly for her lost childhood, those of her sisters, their poverty, her fatigue, the huge roaches in the house, and their inability to fix all of these problems. Her feeling of helplessness set loose a cascade of emotions that had been tucked away. *I need to know what Tony is hiding from me. I can't be in a relationship like this, where I spend more time waiting for him to appear than actually with him.* Hours later, after crying until her eyes hurt and having made an important decision, she fell asleep.

Less than two miles away, Tony wrestled with his pillow and tried to fall asleep. He didn't know how much longer he could keep lying to Olivia. His family was less inquisitive and knew he was always fighting for the cause against the Castro government. He was active among the young Cuban anti-Castro movement, so they hardly asked about his activities. But Olivia was a different case. He was falling in love with her, and his clandestine work with the CIA was hard to explain. It consisted of traveling to the universities and recruiting young Cubans who were against communism and the Castro regime. When recruits signed on, they received a Rolex frogman watch, but they had to be properly trained for their mission, which would involve infiltrating the island and getting things ready for another invasion. They would have to smuggle in arms and ammunition and develop key contacts in the internal subversion (the Bay of Pigs invasion had lacked advance coordination with anti-Casto elements in Cuba).

Tony knew that eventually he would have to travel to Cuba and stay there for weeks at a time. How could he justify this to Olivia? To make things worse, he would have to leave on short notice and wouldn't always be able to say goodbye.

He would soon move into a small apartment in Little Havana. The Agency wanted him there so he could live among other Cubans and make connections. From his debriefings, he learned that some of his neighbors were Castro spies, so he socialized carefully but often. His nightlife was yet another secret he had kept from Olivia. When he said goodnight to her, he claimed he was going home but instead went off to bars and other gathering places on the lively Calle Ocho (Eighth Street) to meet potential leads.

Tossing and turning, he came to no conclusion. But he knew that he did not want to lose Olivia.

The next day, as Olivia was getting home from school, she saw Tony's convertible parked in front of the house. She parked her little Ford Falcon in the pebble driveway, got her books out of the car, and signaled Tony to follow her.

The house was quiet, but soon her mom would get dropped off by a coworker. She picked a spot outside under the tree where there was shade, and Tony dragged the chairs there.

"How are you feeling?" Tony asked.

"I'm too busy to even worry about how I feel," replied Olivia, "but I have made a decision, Tony."

"Before you tell me your decision, I want to tell you that you are right and that I will make an effort to call you when I travel."

Olivia sighed and took a few minutes to gather her thoughts.

"Thank you for saying that, Tony, but this goes far beyond that. I have decided that this is bad timing for us both. And because of the nature of your work, it's probable that things won't change. Furthermore, I don't feel comfortable with your explanation and would like to end this before I lose trust in you completely."

Tony's eyes widened in disbelief. He was speechless. He did not want to lose Olivia, but he didn't know what to say.

After what seemed to Olivia an eternity, she asked, "Do you have anything to say to me?"

Tony still did not talk. He knew she was right. But he could not explain or defend himself.

"Well, Tony," Olivia said, holding back her tears, "Your silence speaks for itself, and I guess that we just need to say goodbye."

"Olivia, wait!" Tony said. "Please trust me. I will explain."

"Explain when, Tony? After your next disappearing act?"

"All I ask is for you to trust me and give me a few days to explain. I need you to trust me on this, Olivia. It's not what you think."

"Tony, please leave. Call me tomorrow, but I need to go inside now." She ran into the house holding back her tears.

Olivia cried in her bed all afternoon. She heard her mother in the kitchen and Mari coming in, but she stayed in her room. Mari called out to her and opened the door to her room twice, but she pretended to be asleep. Learning that Tony had no explanation for his actions confirmed her worst fears. He had been lying, and that's why he couldn't explain. She did not want a dishonest boyfriend, but realizing that she couldn't be with him hurt deeply. She was in love with him. *Trust me*, he had said. How could she trust him if she knew he was lying? Tears kept coming until she fell asleep. Mari knew something was wrong. Olivia would never fall asleep without doing her classwork.

Mari sneaked into her bedroom one last time before going to bed. "Olivia, what's wrong?" she whispered. "Is it Tony?"

"It's over, Mari," Olivia whispered back as tears rolled down her cheek again.

Mari attempted to dry her sister's tears, but Olivia pushed her back. Mari rolled down the sheets and got in the bed with her. She hugged Olivia tightly because she couldn't stand to see her sister so upset. Then Mari started crying and waited until Olivia fell back asleep before she went to her bed.

Early the next morning, Mari went into the kitchen to boil milk and make coffee. She made toast in the red toaster and took a mug of café con leche and warm, buttery toast to Olivia. Mari left the plate by the bed and hurried out. The Tigertail bus came at 6:45 a.m., and if she didn't walk fast enough, she would miss it and be late to school. On the way to school, Mari talked to God again. She first apologized for asking for His help so often and then made another petition. Like her mom said, He had big shoulders and could bear their weight.

Olivia sipped at her warm café con leche and couldn't help but smile at Mari's little ways. She had drawn a heart on the napkin. Then she remembered Tony, and the smile faded. She wiped her tears with the back of her hand and quickly got up. She couldn't go to class without finishing her essay, so she got out her notebook and started writing. About an hour later, she showered and dressed and drove off to school. Being tardy was better than showing up to literature class without the essay. She would finish the rest of her algebra homework in between periods. She kept seeing Tony's frozen face and hearing the tremble in his voice. He was a liar, and, as such, he was out of her life. No more crying, she resolved.

The next couple of days went by slowly, and Olivia didn't hear from Tony. The pain felt like a dagger in her chest, but she was determined to forget him. On the third day, when the bell rang, she got into her Falcon and drove home as usual. Much to her surprise, Tony's car was in front of the house, and her heart started to beat wildly. She wanted to ignore him, but he quickly opened the passenger-side door and got in.

"Olivia, please sit with me, please. I want to explain."

She was going to say no, but the seriousness of his tone left no room for that. She took her books inside the house and signaled for him to follow her to the chairs under the mango tree. Tony handed Olivia a yellow rose he had in his shirt pocket and started speaking slowly and in a low voice.

He told her about his dreams of a free Cuba and how he needed to do something to help liberate his father. He admitted the truth about his job and told her about reenlisting with the CIA. His new operation involved infiltrating Cuba, and he would be gone for weeks sometimes. He would report back to the US so they could prepare for a new invasion. Swearing Olivia to secrecy, he continued.

"You understand that I've told you all this because I don't want to lose you, but if anyone finds out I will end up dead. The worst thing is that we will never know if the CIA or Castro's spies did it. You can't tell anyone in your family—not even your shadow—because it will cost me my life."

Olivia could not speak. She was in shock, and her heart was pounding.

Tony continued. "When I leave, I won't be able to tell you. You'll only find out that I'm gone if I haven't called you for a few days."

Then he told her about his nighttime activities and his new apartment.

"I am glad that I moved away from home," he said. "This way my mother won't worry if I have to leave in the middle of the night. They just send word, and I go. I might have an hour or two to get ready, but I cannot contact you or say anything."

Olivia was dazed. *How could this be happening?* "This is what you were doing instead of selling encyclopedias?" she asked.

"Yes," he said. Then he grabbed both her hands.

"Olivia, I'm not asking you to stay with me. I will understand completely if you want out of this relationship. What lies ahead is dangerous, and you should not be dragged into it. I just love you too much and had some hope that you might still want to be with me. Cuba will soon be free and then my missions will stop. I'll only put my life in danger for a short while." Then he added, "Right now, I'm just happy that I got this off my chest, and that I don't have to lie to you anymore. I trust you so much, I have just placed my life in your hands. Please, just think about it for a couple of days. I will call you or see you in two days."

He kissed her and walked to his car without looking back. He realized that this could be the last time he saw her. But this was all he could do. Their future was in her hands now. In a few days, he would know her answer.

Olivia sat motionless, letting it all sink in. She could hardly breathe, and she started sweating. *What was she going to do? Tony's life was in danger and had been this whole time? How could she be in a relationship like this?* Panic overcame her, and she let out the tears. Luckily, no one was home, but Mari would be there soon.

Mari walked into the house, put her books in her bedroom, and went to the kitchen rolling up her sleeves. Mami would be home soon to start dinner, and Mari needed to do the breakfast dishes. She started the water and then caught a glimpse of Olivia sitting outside with her back to the kitchen window. Olivia's shoulders were shaking, so Mari knew she was crying. Mari dried her hands and rushed outside.

"Olivia, what's wrong?"

"Nothing Mari. I'll be OK in a minute."

"But look at you! You look as if someone has died."

"Will a broken heart qualify?"

"That jerk, Tony. What did he do now?"

Olivia sat up, realizing she must watch her words carefully. Not only did she have to make a decision about the relationship, but she also had to stay quiet about Tony's work. He had trusted her, and she could never betray him. His life was at stake.

She turned her head away from Mari as she lied: "He told me that he was not going to leave his encyclopedia job and that he would keep traveling."

"What are you hiding from me, Olivia?"

"Nothing, Mari, I always tell you everything. I just have a decision to make. I can let him go or spend my days waiting for him to come back from his trips. I love him a lot and don't want to be without him."

"I know you will make the right decision, Olivia, but don't lose hope. He might get tired of all the traveling and change jobs." Mari hugged Olivia before going back to the dishes.

That evening, Enriqueta was tired and went to bed after a light snack. Mari and Olivia ate the leftover beef stew and watched TV together.

"I need to finish my homework," Mari said to Olivia. "Do you want me to stay with you for a while?"

"No thank you, Mari. I'm going to bed."

They hugged, and Olivia felt a warmth run through her. Mari had so much love to give. She hoped that someday Mari would find a good boyfriend who wouldn't make her cry.

The next two days went by quickly. Olivia got teary eyed and felt her chest tighten every time she thought of Tony. Even her dad noticed something was wrong, but she told everyone that she thought she was getting a cold. Two days later, Tony was parked in front of the house after school waiting for Olivia. Her heart raced, and her hands turned cold. They both got out of their cars. At six feet two inches tall, he looked bigger than life. His face was pale as he walked towards her with his arms extended.

"I've missed you," he said in a deep voice. "These have been the longest two days of my life."

Olivia started sobbing in his arms as he pressed her to his chest. Neither wanted to let go. Finally, she pushed away gently to look into his eyes.

"If something happened to you, I couldn't bear it, Tony. This is too dangerous."

"Olivia, I'm not going to war. I'll be going in and making contacts and then reporting back via telegraph. I have been studying and practicing Morse code all this time, and that's my main job. We have safe houses and places to hide on the island, and I won't be alone."

"How will you get in and out?" she asked, calm now. "Through Guantanamo Base?"

"Guantanamo is off limits. Cuba is open water with beaches and inlets everywhere. The agency has already established areas that are too remote to be patrolled. They would never put us at risk. They've been doing this for a while with no problems."

"Tony, I don't know if I can handle this. I'm trying to support you, but I don't know if I can. I will have to see."

"I'm leaving in a few days. I don't know exactly what day. But knowing there's some hope for us makes all the difference in the world."

"You're starting so soon. When will you come back?"

"I've been training for months. I'm one of their best telegraph operators, and they're counting on me and my 'charm' to convince the farmers to join us. These guajiros are forced to work in their fields while their food is being rationed. They need someone to tell them the truth. It's time for Cubans to retake their island."

Olivia said nothing.

He continued. "It's not a war, so don't be scared. I'll be back before you know it. Please remember not to tell anyone, not even my mother."

He took the car keys out of his pocket.

"Are you leaving so soon?" Olivia asked with a shaky voice.

Tony gestured for Olivia to follow him into his car. They sat and talked, and she cried. They spoke about what he had been doing and how hard it had been to keep it a secret. She admitted how relieved she was that he had not been lying, although now she preferred the lie to this danger. Tony understood, and she felt closer to him than ever. Later, when it was time to say goodbye, they hugged and kissed passionately.

"I will never leave you, Tony," she said. "Come back fast and safe. I will be waiting for you." She spoke with such strength and calmness that she didn't recognize her voice.

Tony's face lit up, and he hugged her again.

"Thank you, Olivia, for trusting me and being by my side. You have no idea how happy it makes me."

Olivia stood on the sidewalk waving goodbye at Tony. Her love and pride for him were immeasurable. She wasn't crying. A feeling of peace and resolve had taken over. Standing there she felt the strength of their love. He was the bravest person she knew, and she would be by his side while he risked his life for his people. Their people. *Our love is bigger than our fear*, she decided.

That night the phone rang, and Olivia ran to pick it up. Tony would always call to say goodnight. They talked about their love but avoided discussing his activities. Before they hung up, Olivia couldn't help but ask a question: "Tony, are you scared?"

He paused before he answered. "Not anymore," he replied. "The only thing that scares me is losing you."

Then they said goodnight.

The next morning, Olivia felt strangely happy. A weight had been lifted from her shoulders. Mari was having breakfast and looked up when Olivia walked in. Mari noticed the glow on Olivia's face.

"You look radiant today. What happened? Did you make up with Tony?"

"Yes. Tony and I are fine."

"Is he going to quit that stupid encyclopedia gig?"

"No Mari, he's not. I'm just going to support him in whatever he is doing. That's what you do when you really love someone. And I love him very much."

"He doesn't know how lucky he is," Mari said. "I have to go, or I'll miss my bus." She ran to get her bookbag and waved goodbye from the door.

Olivia sat sipping at her café con leche. Her school started a little later than Mari's and was on the opposite end of the city. She liked having a few minutes to herself every morning and sat silently. Her mom was already at work, and her dad was sleeping because he had finished his shift at 3 a.m. and would head to his other job later that morning. So she spent the time thinking of Tony and replaying their conversation in her mind. Time flew, and she didn't have time to shower. She dressed, grabbed her books, and locked the door behind her. As she was approaching her car, she spotted something on her windshield. It was a yellow rose, her favorite. He must have passed by early and left it. How she wished she could have seen him. She would thank him later after school. She held the rose, and a thorn pricked her finger.

That afternoon, as she turned the corner into her street, Tony's car wasn't there waiting. She felt disappointed but went inside to call him. The phone rang but no one answered. So she started with her homework and waited for her mother and Mari to come home. Soon her mother was cooking dinner, and the smell led her to the kitchen.

"Hi, Mami," she said brightly. "What's for dinner? I'm starving."

"That's good to hear, *mijita*. You haven't had much appetite lately." Enriqueta smiled at her.

"Well, today I'm hungry."

"Good, because I'm making one of your favorites. *Picadillo*."

Mari came in with her usual excitement and abundance of stories. Lorenzo arrived and went to the bedroom to nap before his night shift. The house smelled of family and love. Enriqueta, who usually napped after coming home from work, seemed energized that evening. The three women sat down to have dinner together. They laughed and told more stories before Enriqueta read them the latest letter from Lucia. It said she had met a "very nice young man" and that they were now dating.

"How exciting!" Mari shouted. "I'm going to ask her to send a picture of him. I'll write her tonight and ask her."

Mari got up and took the dishes to the kitchen and then went to her room to write Lucia. Enriqueta said goodnight, and Olivia sat by the TV waiting for Tony's call. It was *Candid Camera* night, and she lay on the couch to watch. The voices faded, and she fell asleep. She woke up to off-air TV static and checked her watch. It was 2 a.m. Tony hadn't called. *Maybe he had come home late and didn't want to wake us up*, she thought. She now understood why he stayed out late sometimes roaming the streets of Little Havana. Restless, she took a warm shower and went to bed. She'd find out tomorrow. Praying, she fell asleep and woke up earlier than usual.

In the afternoon, his car was not there. That next night he didn't call, and then she knew. He was gone. The yellow rose had been his goodbye.

8

El Perro ya Llegó

After a two-day debriefing, Tony was dropped off at the departure point. The mother ship was waiting, and it sailed out of the Florida Keys in the early morning hours. The time it would take the ship to navigate the 250 nautical miles from Key West to their destination in Cuba was determined by many factors, including weather and maritime traffic, but the trip usually took one full day. As the ship approached international waters, the crew waited for the all-clear signal. On this trip, Tony was accompanied by another recruiter, and they were bringing assault rifles to the island. The men hefted duffel bags as they boarded a combat reconnaissance craft that would take them to the drop-off point.

They heard a Cuban patrol boat nearby and turned off their motor. When the patrol went elsewhere, the reconnaissance craft continued on and dropped the men at a deserted inlet. They made their way through a mangrove carrying their heavy gear and went farther inland. Tony led the way because he had memorized the map. They made it to the caves, where an agent—who had been waiting for relief—greeted them. They sat, listened to his activity report, and exchanged important information. He thanked them and said goodbye. He needed to get to his pickup point in two hours.

Tony assessed the cave. It was outfitted with a couple of sleeping bags, two shovels, a box filled with fruit, a dozen water jugs, and a makeshift table made of plywood and rocks. A stream nearby served as their water supply. He removed the telegraph from his backpack and sent a transmission: *El Perro ya llegó* (the Dog has arrived). They hid their heavy gear under some piled-up branches and prepared to leave for their next pickup.

Two hours later, the men hid in darkness under a huge jagüey tree near a rural road. A black jeep came down the road and slowed. Its lights flashed, and the men emerged from their hiding spot and walked cautiously toward the jeep.

"Hello, I'm Manuel," the driver said from his open window. "I will take you to meet the others."

Once inside the jeep, they realized that Manuel was wearing a full *miliciano* (militiaman) uniform. Noticing the uniform made them uneasy, and they kept quiet the rest of the drive. Manuel started talking about the weather—rain was coming tomorrow—but thankfully did not ask any questions. They traveled east and arrived at a house in a small town as the sun was starting to rise. The houses in that poor neighborhood looked more like ruins, and this one was out of sight, covered by shady trees and obscured by a crumbling concrete wall. Manuel pushed the iron gate and led them to a door, where a young woman waited. Once inside, Manuel made introductions.

"This is my sister Ana, and two of my brothers," Manuel said. "You'll meet my other two brothers later. You will use this house only in case of emergency, and when they instruct you to meet at the jagüey tree."

Tony realized there were five brothers and one sister but didn't know which of them lived at the house other than Manuel and his sister. He did see some toys scattered on the floor.

Ana gave them breakfast, which consisted of warm café con leche with no sugar, one fried egg, orange juice, and stale bread. She apologized for the condition of the bread and the lack of sugar. She explained that they were lucky to have some hens. Eggs were scarce, and the food-ration card only allowed them one pound of flour a month and one pound of sugar. Tony knew of the food shortage on the island but didn't expect that sugar would be in short supply. The country was rich in sugarcane.

"All the sugar we produce gets sent to Russia," one of the brothers explained.

Manuel rose from the table. "Quickly, we must leave before anyone notices I'm missing. We will talk in the jeep."

The men said goodbye and thanked Ana.

Back at the jeep, Manuel told them that Ana had a small son. Her husband had been shot by a *miliciano* while he was stealing cattle (the family had been hungry and desperate). Ana was resourceful in general and a nurse by trade, so these days she took care of the safe house and looked after family members when they were sick.

Manuel then talked shop with Tony and his partner. He shared the names of a few guajiros he thought might join the cause along with the names of farmers already supportive. Manuel said food would be delivered when possible. He said someone would hang it in the fig tree.

"You'll be lucky if you get one meal a day." Manuel said. "Luckily, you'll find plenty of fruit trees that are still in season."

Tony wrote everything down on a small piece of paper that he folded and slid inside his shoe. Manuel let them out of the jeep at the jagüey tree, where the men plucked some figs before walking back to the cave for some much-needed sleep. The men waited for the next nightfall before leaving the cave. They searched for and found barrels that were hidden nearby and then filled them with the weapons they'd smuggled.

They thought about the days to come. The plan was to head separately to their assigned towns, both in the Oriente province. Each would mingle with farmers in the hope of recruiting those unhappy with the system. The lack of advance recruiting had doomed the Bay of Pigs invasion, and the government didn't want to make the same mistake twice. The current goal was to form small subversive cells throughout the island so that they would be ready for the next invasion. They would have to seek out the guajiros, those who worked the fields at the crack of dawn cutting sugarcane for the government. After the guajiros took dinner, they would usually relax outside their *bohios*, or thatched-roof huts. There, they would enjoy the evening breeze while smoking their freshly rolled cigars. It was the perfect time to engage them in conversation.

The men prepared that night in the cave. They removed the small pieces of paper in their shoes and started memorizing the details. Afterwards, they lit a match and burned the papers. Tony got into his sleeping bag for the night. The ground beneath him was hard, and his body ached from lack of sleep, but thoughts of Olivia kept him company. What was she doing now? He hadn't called for two nights, so she must know he'd left. He didn't know how long this mission would last or if Olivia would go the distance with him. Could she understand his reasons? His father was there in the same country, breathing the same air and looking at the same sky. Tony's every move brought his father closer to freedom. Surely Olivia could appreciate this. His eyes were heavy. He entered a deep sleep within minutes.

9

THE SECRET

Olivia woke up startled. She hadn't slept peacefully since she'd last heard from Tony. That was eight days ago.

Mari was singing in the bathroom. Olivia missed their long talks, but now she avoided them. Mari asked too many questions, and Olivia didn't like answering with lies. As far as Mari knew, Tony was off selling encyclopedias.

On this particular day, a Saturday, Enriqueta was making breakfast—*huevos a la flamenco*. She cooked the eggs in sautéed onions, garlic, tomatoes, and an olive oil base and then baked everything with *sofrito* and petits pois in small tartlet pans. They came out of the oven bubbling.

Mari walked into the kitchen with her nose in the air, as if the aroma was pulling her. "Mami, I can't wait. Thank you for making them today. We're receiving a lot of Christmas merchandise at the store, and I doubt I'll get a break for lunch."

"Please go and get Olivia," Enriqueta answered. "The eggs will get cold."

Olivia, who had caught the aroma, was already sitting at the table. Even Lorenzo came out with his sleepy eyes. "The smell of these eggs could wake up the dead," he declared. "The power of food can't be overestimated."

While everyone ate, he told funny stories about his work. He was trying to cheer up Olivia, and it was working. Lorenzo was a fast eater, and that gave him time to hold court while he finished. On Saturdays, he cleaned offices all day.

At one point, Enriqueta cleared her throat and pulled a letter from the pocket of her apron. Lorenzo knew that look in Enriqueta's eyes. She was about to have a serious talk with the girls. He thanked her for the eggs, kissed everyone goodbye, and left for his janitorial job.

"Olivia," her mother started, "you know that I've been wanting you to continue piano. Yesterday, this letter came in the mail for you."

She reached out and gave Olivia an open envelope. Olivia read it slowly, and a big smile came to her face. Suddenly the smile turned into a frown.

"How come they are giving me a scholarship if they only heard me play once? And I did so badly?"

"You might think you did badly, Olivia, but apparently they don't agree."

"But, Mami, first you wanted ballet and now piano. Why don't you just stop? I can't do this now." By then, Olivia was tearing up. Enriqueta looked incredulous.

"What's wrong with you, Olivia? This has always been your dream, at least until this Tony came along. You don't think I notice how unhappy he's made you? You can't continue this way. You need to get on with your life and let him travel and do whatever he is doing, which I'm sure has nothing to do with encyclopedias!" Enriqueta had let it all out angrily.

Olivia got up and went to her room. Now she was openly sobbing. She couldn't imagine life without Tony and didn't care about a future without him. *Why couldn't her mom understand that she loved him? How could her mom apply for a scholarship without telling her?*

Olivia's long day continued downtown at Schneer's Jewelers, where she received and labeled new items ahead of the Christmas rush. Schneer's normally closed at 7 p.m., but she had to work overtime. Soon they would be open until 9 p.m. to accommodate Christmas shoppers. That night, she knew she wouldn't make it on time to get Mari, so she drove east on Flagler Street with the radio on. She rolled down her window and let the cool autumn air caress her face. She was thankful that her workday had been busy because otherwise she would have gone mad. She would have thought about the fight with her mom all day. How could she explain to her mother that starting piano again would consume all her time? She needed time for Tony and time to think, not the pressure of piano.

It was past 9:30 p.m. when she got home, and the house was dark. She opened the front door and turned on the small entry light. Then she put some lights on. Mari was not home yet, so she went to her mother's bedroom. It was dark, but Enriqueta turned in her bed.

"Mami, can I speak to you?" Olivia asked.

"I'm very sleepy, Olivia," Enriqueta said. "We'll speak tomorrow."

Olivia changed into her pajamas and got into bed. Soon Mari would be home. She'd wait to see how her day had been. Olivia's eyes were heavy. Within minutes, she was sound asleep. She wouldn't hear Mari call out her name.

The next morning Olivia woke up and got dressed for Mass. Enriqueta, already dressed, waited for her in the living room. Mari was too tired and would sleep in.

On the way to St. Michael's Catholic Church, Olivia started explaining to Enriqueta that she was not in the right frame of mind to dedicate herself to piano. She chose her words carefully to avoid hurting Enriqueta's feelings while not revealing anything about Tony's activities.

After Olivia finished speaking, Enriqueta cleaned the lenses of her eyeglasses as she usually did before a serious conversation.

"Olivia, I understand everything you say. But all I ask from you is one thing."

"And what is that, Mami?" Olivia dreaded the answer.

"That you go to the conservatory to meet the director and see what they have to offer."

"But, Mami, what good will that do?"

"I expect you to do at least that."

Olivia knew the conversation was over, and they arrived at church.

At Mass, the smell of the incense and the sound of the church's organ soothed Olivia. She prayed for Tony: "Oh God, please let Tony be safe and come back to me soon."

That was all she could do, pray for him. She also prayed for God to give her strength. She didn't know if she could follow through on her promise to support him indefinitely. These last 10 days had been a struggle.

The offerings basket was passed through the pews, and she thought of their church in Havana. It seemed a lifetime ago. She and Enriqueta each contributed a dollar. The rest of Mass went by quickly, and Olivia never stopped praying for Tony. Maybe he could hear her calling out his name—wherever he was.

The rest of Sunday was spent cleaning the house and taking the clothes to the laundromat. That afternoon, Enriqueta would rest and recharge for the busy week of work and school ahead. She had decided to get her degree in pharmacology. She went to class one night a week and met with a study group two nights.

Olivia took laundromat duty. Time passed slowly as she rotated loads. Finally she got to the sheets. She was folding the last one when she felt a tug on one corner. Was someone trying to help her? Leery of strangers, she lowered the sheet and prepared to send the helper away.

Tony stood before her. "Tony!"

She started sobbing. The sheet fell to the floor as they hugged tightly. Then she started kissing his face while he caressed her hair. The other customers watched in surprise.

"When did you get in?" Olivia asked him. "Why didn't you call me?"

Tony put a finger to her lips. "I'm here, and I'm fine."

He helped Olivia finish folding, and they brought the clothes to her car. Before long they were sitting in the living room. The air was thick with the scent of Pine Sol. Mari asked a lot of questions.

"How many encyclopedias did you sell? Is it worth it? Why can't you sell in Miami?"

Mari wore them out.

"We're going to get ice cream." Olivia said.

Tony put the convertible top down so they could enjoy the cool, starry evening. Olivia felt like the luckiest woman in the world. As they snuggled, she forgot all the pain and suffering caused by his absence. No questions were asked and no explanations given.

"I love you, Olivia," Tony whispered in her ear.

"I love you more." Olivia answered. "Will you be staying long?"

"I don't know the answer to that question, and I don't think I ever will."

Later that night, Olivia came home and went straight to bed. The same relentless streetlight shining in her face made her smile. She was so happy that Tony was back. *Christmas is six weeks away. I'm sure Tony won't have to travel during the holidays.* This was her favorite time of year, and Tony was back. All was well.

"You won't keep me up tonight," she told the light as she turned to the other side.

Once again, she confirmed that her love for Tony was greater than her fears.

10

WHERE DO THE DUCKS GO?

Lucia was coming home for Thanksgiving, and we had finally moved to a bigger house just across the street. It had one more bedroom and one more bathroom. The garage had been converted into a small apartment, which allowed us to provide temporary housing to family arriving from Cuba. My father planned to get bunkbeds for it.

Tony helped us paint the new house, and Olivia came rushing home from school every day to accompany him. They were together every minute except when she had to go to school. To make more time for Tony, Olivia asked for fewer hours at the jewelry store. Her boss wasn't happy, but he accommodated the request. He let her trade Friday night for another weeknight, and she worked on Saturdays from 9 a.m. to 9 p.m. The conservatory was no longer a topic of discussion. Enriqueta now had more contact with Tony, and she started to like him. She realized that Olivia was madly in love with him, and her daughter's happiness was more important to her than anything else.

On Tuesday evening, Olivia and I went to the airport to greet Lucia. I had made a "Welcome Home" sign and carried it with me to the gate. Lucia walked into the airport terminal with a big smile on her face and her arms wide open. Her hair was cut short, and she wore a wool black-and-white checkered beret with a matching scarf. So bohemian, I thought, so New York. We jumped for joy like schoolgirls until we realized that we were blocking the gate.

At home, Enriqueta was beaming. Lucia told us stories of New York and how she had met her boyfriend, Richard, who was studying law and had an internship at one of the biggest entertainment law firms in Manhattan. She brought plenty of pictures of Richard, her roommate Marcy, her teachers, and her cat Lola. She was also working part time at the Met and talked about its current exhibits and the ones soon to come.

"Are you happy in New York, Lucia?" Olivia asked her.

"I miss you all so much, but my future is there," she said. "If I am going to accomplish anything with my music, I need to stay there. Rick's cousin is the agent of the Sherman Brothers, and he wants me to meet them. They write music for famous singers and movies."

We talked into the night and went through all her pictures. New York looked different from when we had last gone with our parents. There were more buildings and billboards. Juilliard looked old, but it had character. We all fell asleep in one small bed until Olivia slipped away to her room.

We had a memorable Thanksgiving Day. My father had asked Olivia to invite Tony's mom and brother, but his mother preferred to host a quiet meal at home with immediate family. She believed celebrations would have to wait until her husband was free again, which I found honorable. Tony came after their meal and ate twice. We all played bingo, betting pennies and dimes. Then came charades. I did my Charlie Chaplin imitation, Olivia did Marilyn Monroe, Lucia did Judy Garland, and Tony did Marlon Brando. Soon we were all singing—songs in Spanish with pots and pans for the beat, along with songs in English with a harmonica brought by Lucia. Then my father got up and started singing the national hymn of Cuba and started to tear up. We all took turns hugging him.

Lucia told him, "Don't worry, Papi, I think we will be back next year."

After that, everyone was more pensive but still happy. I loved this new holiday that the US had given us. Cuba had nothing like it. Most holidays there were religious in nature, particularly Catholic, and traced to our Spanish ancestry. Some people consider Thanksgiving a secular holiday, but no religious holiday except Holy Week ever made me feel closer to God, nor did I ever dream of eating such a delicious meal. Stuffing and cranberry jelly were my favorites. "I must write a poem about Thanksgiving," I told Olivia that night.

Lucia left on Sunday night, and we were all sad. All except my mother. She told us that we needed to let Lucia go, that she was born to write music just as we were born to do something special. I wondered what I wanted to do in my future. Writing was what I loved the most, but I also wanted to help my parents with money, which seemed impossible with poetry. I was starting high school the following year and needed to think about my future. Then I thought of Olivia. *Will she really quit piano? Maybe she can be a piano teacher! I will ask her tomorrow.*

I didn't have a chance to ask her the next morning, because she was asleep when I left for school. I went to the school library during my free period to look up poetry careers and came out more confused. I read the phrase "poets don't make any money" several times. When I came across a painting called *The Poor Poet* by the German romanticist Carl Spitzweg, I decided to stop the search. Unlike poets, pianists could make money. They played with orchestras and toured the world. Olivia could have a beautiful life. Tony would surely support her if he loved her.

The school day went by fast. It turned cloudy, so I raced to the bus after school and prayed for the rain to hold off. Just as I got off the transfer bus and started my walk home, the rain started. I didn't have the poncho that Olivia had bought me, so I pulled my sweater over my head and sloshed through the puddles. The rain seeped through the soles of my flats, and by the time I got home, my feet were wrinkled and stained black from shoe paint. I draped my wet clothes on the chair of my bedroom and removed the soaked cardboard from my shoes before hopping in the shower. *I'll fix the shoes tomorrow. I have more cardboard, and in the meantime I'll wear my summer white flats.*

Enriqueta was sitting on the couch with Tony as I came in rubbing my hair dry with a towel.

Before I could say hello, she addressed me. "Mari, can you please give us a few minutes. I'm having a conversation with Tony."

I went back to my room, and whispering voices trailed behind me. I didn't know what they were talking about, but I was sure that Olivia didn't know about their conversation. I wouldn't bring it up either.

A few minutes later, Olivia's car pulled up, and Enriqueta walked to the kitchen. I peeked out and saw Olivia kissing Tony.

***

On December 2, 1961, Castro finally admitted the truth about his ideology in a television program: "I am a Marxist-Leninist and shall be one until the end of my life. Marxism or scientific socialism has become the revolutionary movement of the working class." By then, he had the full military and economic backing of the Soviet Union. My father started talking about the announcement as soon as he came home from work. It stirred up all the emotions he had tried to control for so long. All Cuban exiles had known this day would come—when Castro would finally admit having lied to Cubans for two years. Nevertheless, the news was hard to take.

Life continued as usual at our house. Olivia came home from school one day and changed into a nice dress. She put on earrings and some lipstick and then pinched her cheeks for color. She walked out of her room to join Enriqueta, who waited in the living room.

"Where are you going?" I asked.

"To the conservatory," Enriqueta answered with a wink.

That was great news! Maybe my sister had had a change of heart.

More exciting news came only days later. The week was over, and Christmas vacation would start in just three days, when my mother asked, "How would you girls like to go and spend Christmas with Lucia in New York?"

I screeched and Olivia cried, "Yes!" Enriqueta wouldn't be going. She said she needed to rest and study, and our father had to work. But I knew that we were short money and that Lucia couldn't come for Christmas because she was working on a composition due in January. "That will be your Christmas present," she added. "You will stay with Lucia and her roommate in her New York apartment."

The three days went by slowly, but finally we were walking down the corridors of the Miami International Airport Terminal. As we did, I started feeling nauseated and looked for Olivia's eyes. She immediately understood. Silently, I slipped my hand in hers.

"Don't worry, Mari. Nothing is going to happen. We are in the US and those things don't happen here," she said reassuringly. But I wasn't really listening. I was sweating heavily, and Olivia noticed, so we stopped at a vending machine, and she bought a Coke.

"Drink this. It will make you feel better," she said, lifting my ponytail and dabbing the back of my neck with a tissue.

The panic had caught me by surprise, but eventually I composed myself and we continued on toward the gate. When we were finally sitting in our seats, I let out a big sigh.

"It seems like ages ago that we left Havana, and yet it has only been two years," I said. "Do you think we will have to return?"

"Probably," she whispered.

I sat by the window and looked out during takeoff. The green of Miami below was beautiful.

"Why are you smiling?" Olivia asked.

"I hadn't noticed how many palm trees there are in Miami. It's just like Havana, only they are smaller."

"The difference is that ours are the royal palms. They're majestic and a lot taller."

Outside the terminal in New York, Olivia held an envelope.

"You have money for two taxi rides," Enriqueta had said. "To and from the airport." Olivia signaled for a taxi, and one pulled up. We got in, and she gave the driver Olivia's address. After we fought afternoon traffic, we finally entered Manhattan. It looked like a scene from a Christmas postcard, with lights and decorations everywhere. In the past, on our way to and from our summer camp, the city air was hot and thick with fumes. Now it was cold, and the scent of pine—from Christmas trees being sold by street vendors—filled the air.

In Miami, you had to go shopping downtown to see Christmas lights. Few people decorated their homes. We didn't have a tree, but we did put up a Nativity set. My mom had salvaged it from our looted home in Havana. I thought of our baby Jesus and its beautiful face. Back in Havana, it would take my mother days to finish our Nativity scene. It had mountains made of brown paper, painted streams, mirrors meant to be lakes, shrubs, moss, sheep, and *pastores*. The manger was made of twigs and wood, and all the figures, which her mother had brought from Spain, were made of exquisite Spanish porcelain. This beautiful spectacle took residence in our home through the Feast of the Epiphany, better known as Three Kings Day among the children.

The taxi driver's voice brought me back to my reality. He announced we had arrived at our location on Delancey Street on the Lower East Side. I looked around and saw an old, run-down brick building. The driver pointed to a bridge in the distance.

"That's the Williamsburg Bridge," he said in his heavy Brooklyn accent. "They tried to make it look like the Eiffel Tower, but I've never seen the Eiffel Tower so I wouldn't know."

My sister took money from the envelope and put it back in a secret compartment of her purse. When I opened the taxi door, cold air slapped me in the face. It was the coldest weather I had ever experienced. We wore wool coats but could hardly move.

"Olivia!" I called out shivering.

Olivia came to me with an extra wool scarf that our father had given her and wrapped it around my neck and mouth.

We lugged weekend bags—filled with belongings and presents from Enriqueta—to the door and pressed a button marked "Salomon" (the last name of Lucia's roommate). Quickly, we heard a buzzer and opened the door. It was warmer inside, thank God. We started up the stairs toward the fourth floor and heard Lucia's voice calling us as we got closer. She met us halfway down with hugs and kisses and then helped us with our bags.

"Was the flight OK?" she asked. "Did you bring heavy sweaters? Are you staying the whole week?" She was short of breath and stopped at a landing on the second floor. "I've taken off Sunday, and I'm off half of Monday since the museum closes early for Christmas Eve."

Christmas fell on a Tuesday, and Lucia wanted us to stay until Sunday, but our mother had set up our return flight for Wednesday. She worried about the cost of meals and said four days was plenty. She did want us to spend *Noche Buena*, or Christmas Eve, with Lucia. The tradition featured a feast of pit-roasted pork, black beans, and rice. In Cuba, the entire family came to our house for the meal, which included roast suckling pig. When everyone finished eating, all the women would go to the *Misa del Gallo*, or Midnight Mass, while most of the men stayed at home and played dominoes.

Once inside the apartment, we set our bags down and met Lucia's roommate Marcy. Olivia took in the open space of the studio and took her gloves off. I started talking to Marcy.

Lucia got our attention: "We're lucky to have a good radiator to warm us. I'll show you how to turn it down when you leave."

I couldn't help but notice that it was a clunky, archaic-looking silver box under the window and wondered if it really worked.

"That's our desk and also dining table," Lucia said, following Olivia's eyes.

Lucia and Marcy each had beds on opposite sides of the main room. Marcy had a Murphy bed that pulled out from an armoire.

The rest of her area was taken up with several guitar cases and music stands. On the other side, Lucia had a double bed, a comfortable armchair, an ottoman she had salvaged from a neighbor, and a small piano. Lucia called it a pianet and said her professor was letting her borrow it to practice.

Lucia pulled out a thick sleeping bag from under her bed. "Mari, if all three of us are not comfortable in the double bed, would you mind sleeping in this? It belongs to Rick, and he dropped it off last night in case we would need it."

"Of course, Luci," I said. "It looks comfortable."

Marcy announced that she had made pasta for us. The smell of garlic had my mouth watering. Olivia and I looked at each other wide-eyed. We hadn't eaten any real food since breakfast, and our bones yearned for something warm.

"Thank you," Lucia and I said at the same time.

Lucia cleared the textbooks from the table and put them in a box underneath filled with other books and notebooks. Then she put four mats decorated with poinsettias on the table.

"I bought them yesterday just for you," she said proudly.

We sat down and said a prayer of thanks before digging into the delicious pasta. Lucia and Marcy talked about New York and how different it was to live there. Marcy was from Ohio, so she was used to the weather. After the meal, everyone helped with dishes and wiped the table.

"If you don't mind," I said, "I want to curl up in that comfy looking sleeping bag. I'm exhausted."

"I could sleep too," Olivia said, "but I want to catch up with Luci and hear about Rick."

They continued talking on a small couch near the crusty radiator.

***

Olivia had trouble sleeping. She lay next to Lucia looking at the ceiling of the studio. The hissing and bubbling noise from the radiator, the traffic noise, and thoughts of Tony kept her eyes open. She thought of how happy and supportive he had been about her trip to New York. She had been the hesitant one. She feared he'd be gone when she got back to Miami.

"Don't think about that," he said. "Just go to New York and enjoy yourself. Lucia needs the company, and it's only four days. Besides, you can't plan your life around when you think they might call. We just need to take every day as it comes."

The night before she left for New York, she and Tony had gone out for pizza to celebrate Christmas. They exchanged gifts and talked about their lives. Tony asked her to think more about attending the conservatory.

"Nothing would make me happier than to see you continue with piano," he said. "If it's something you love, you should think more about it on your trip."

His selfless words reassured her that she had fallen in love with the right person. She finally drifted off to sleep.

***

The next day, Lucia woke us up bright and early.

"Rise and shine," she said. "Rick brought us bagels from the deli."

Marcy stayed in bed. She had the covers over her head and was dead to the world.

"She is a heavy sleeper," Lucia said.

Rick was kind and well mannered. He couldn't keep his eyes off Lucia. They had met at the museum's gift shop, where Lucia worked, and had been dating for two months.

"You need to hear your sister's new music," he said with pride.

We devoured the bagels and thanked Rick.

Lucia said Rick would be leaving for the day. "He wants to give us our time alone, but he's going to try to rejoin us for dinner."

We dressed and went exploring. Lucia bought us ferry tickets to the Statue of Liberty and Ellis Island, and we boarded soon after.

When we arrived at the Statue of Liberty, the attendants gave us a map. We thought we would go up to the top of the statue but saw the cost and decided to stay at the pedestal. We admired the beautiful architecture at the statue's base and then headed to

Ellis Island and its museum, where America's immigration history is chronicled and brought to life. The Immigrant Wall of Honor impressed me the most, and I realized that our own diaspora resembled that of others who'd passed through the island. The view of Manhattan on that clear, crisp day was breathtaking.

After our return trip on the ferry, we returned to the apartment where Lucia made us some delicious hot chocolate. I asked if we could go to a hot dog stand.

"Better yet, I'll take you to *the* hot dog stand. Do you remember the hotdogs we had at Coney Island? We can get them nearby at a stand that just opened."

Walking for what seemed an eternity, we finally reached the Nathan's stand. The place was swarming with people, but we eventually made it to the front to order. We each got hot dogs and Cokes. I ate mine slowly to savor it. That simple meal hit the spot for all of us.

The walk back to the apartment seemed shorter on a full stomach. Still, I longed to go to Central Park and sit by the lagoon.

That evening, Rick picked us up in a taxi and took us to Junior's restaurant.

"I heard from Lucia that you both love cheesecake. They have the best in town. All the food is great—just leave some room for the cheesecake."

Olivia and I looked at each other wondering if we'd have to dip into some of the taxi money meant for the airport trip. And we didn't know how expensive this Junior's was. We checked the menu for prices.

"I'm still full from the hot dog," I said.

Rick whispered into Lucia's ear, and she turned around.

"Rick is paying tonight," she said. "It's his Christmas present."

Olivia put up some resistance, but Rick wasn't having it. Olivia and I shared a club sandwich and a slice of cheesecake. After a lovely dinner, we took a stroll outside the restaurant. The cold air cut it short, and Rick hailed us a cab.

The next day, we went shopping for the Christmas Eve meal that evening. Olivia stopped at the public phone booth in the corner and tried to call Tony, but there was no answer. We went to a neighborhood market and bought groceries. Lucia cooked black beans while Olivia baked pork loin. I cooked white rice, which came out sticky. Then I remembered having come across a crop of red wildflowers on a neighboring block, so I left the apartment with scissors in my pocket. I brought back a handful and placed them in a glass next to the poinsettia on the dining table.

The meal was delightful, and afterwards Lucia went to the pianet to play her latest pieces. Olivia and I sat in awe and couldn't help but cry. Like all great music, Lucia's compositions awakened emotions once safely tucked away. Each note seemed to stir more feeling. We had missed Lucia more than we knew.

On Christmas day, Lucia brought Olivia to the dorms early so she could call Tony. Olivia was able to speak with him and wish him a merry Christmas. She was on a high when she took me to Central Park that afternoon. As we watched the ducks, I recalled *Catcher in the Rye*, which I had just read. Like Holden Caufield, I felt an unexplainable longing and sadness. How do the ducks make it through winter? Where is their real home, here or where they migrate? Only a few Mallards waddled about the cold lagoon. The others must have gone south.

We left New York later that day, just before a big snowstorm would hit NYC. In three hours, we went from 38 degrees to 77 degrees. Our bones were warmer and our hearts fuller. Our Lucia, our dear Luci, was well and happy. Her future seemed as vibrant as the Miami sun.

11

MALARIA

Olivia sat at the edge of the bed reading the note: *Missing you. Hope you had a good time. I'll see you soon.* She felt desperate.

When had he left the note, yesterday or this morning? She must have missed him by a few hours. His last words had been "See you soon." She couldn't stop wondering when he'd left or where he was. She didn't have school because of Christmas break, so all she could do was think. She looked for Mari that evening.

"I didn't get you a Christmas present," she said. "What would you like to do tomorrow?"

"Don't worry about presents, Olivia. We used all our money on the trip."

"If you had money, what would you want?"

"The only thing I want is something that is free. A puppy from the dog pound."

"Have you talked it over with Mami and Papi?"

"Not really, not lately. I told Papi when we first got here, and he said that we didn't have enough money for our own food, let alone food for a dog."

"But things have changed, Mari. Now there are two salaries, plus we work."

"It's OK, Olivia. Why don't we go see a movie instead? I've been wanting to see *Pocketful of Miracles* with Bette Davis. Her daughter thinks she is a rich socialite, but she's a beggar who sells apples. Luci said she saw it with Rick and that it was wonderful."

They decided to catch the matinee the next day. Mari had wanted to sleep in, but Olivia woke her up. She rushed Mari out the door and into the Falcon.

"Olivia, it's not even 11, and the matinee doesn't start until noon. Why are we going so early?"

"It's a good movie and it just came out," Olivia responded. "There might be a line."

Mari turned the radio on and looked for a song. She found Bobby Vee's "Take Good Care of My Baby" and started singing happily. Suddenly, she noticed Olivia's teary eyes.

"What's wrong, Olivia?"

"Please turn that off," Olivia said. "Everything reminds me of Tony and that he's not here with me."

Mari turned the radio off quickly. "Sorry, Olivia. Don't cry, he's probably missing you too. He'll be back before you know it. This is the busiest season for a salesman."

They talked about how lucky they were to have the week off from school and work, and the conversation carried on until Olivia stopped the car. Mari realized they were not downtown, where the theater was.

"Where are we?" Mari asked. Then she saw the sign to her right: Humane Society Animal Shelter.

"What? Are we getting a puppy?" Mari shrieked with delight. "Does Mami know?"

"Yes, I cleared it with her," said Olivia. "She says it's OK as long as you take full responsibility for it."

At the shelter, they looked at dogs and puppies of all sizes. Mari wanted to take them all. Olivia watched the happiness in her face and couldn't help but feel happy herself. That was Mari's gift— the joy she always managed to have. Mari made her laugh, which boosted Olivia's mood.

Mari took every dog out of the cage to pet and hug them. Finally, she picked one. It wasn't a puppy. It was a middle-aged cocker spaniel. She was brown and shiny, and her sad eyes had pierced their hearts. She reminded them of Suzy, their cocker spaniel in Cuba.

"Yes Mari, I like your pick. I loved her from the minute I saw her."

The dog already had a name, Gypsy, so they decided to keep it. Gypsy was a shy and cuddly dog, and the shelter estimated her age at 4 or 5 years. She was housebroken and spayed, so she was ready to come home with them.

The rest of the week Gypsy occupied everyone's attention. Even Enriqueta liked her and thought she was a good choice. Olivia was happy she had helped grant Mari's Christmas wish. They went together to the pet store to buy Gypsy a leash and collar, and Mari took her for long walks. Soon Gypsy became a permanent member of the family. Olivia and Mari gave her all the love and attention she had lacked.

***

On January 1, 1962, the Freedom Tower opened its doors in downtown Miami to help Cubans seeking political asylum in the US. There, exiles could have their alien or exile visas processed. Clerks provided all the paperwork they needed to file. The office also provided food assistance to needy exile families. I realized the magnitude of the Cuban exodus and thought of Ellis Island. How lucky we were to be in the US! The country had greeted us with open arms and had become our home. I didn't want to live in any other place, not even in Cuba, although I couldn't say that to my father. The thought of returning triggered anxiety and strengthened my attachment to the US—its symbols and traditions. I made a mental note to ask Olivia where I could get an American flag.

***

Our week off school had gone by fast, and school resumed in January. There was still no sign of Tony. Another week went by, and then another. Julio, one of Tony's friends, came by the house to see

Olivia. She had no idea why he was there, but after some small talk, he told Olivia that Tony was hospitalized with malaria and that he would contact her when he could. Anxious, she asked Julio a lot of questions but received no answers. Olivia then realized that Julio also worked for the CIA. *How many of them worked for the agency?* she wondered. The males in her generation were putting their lives at risk to free Cuba. She was proud of Tony, but worrying about him was torture.

Two more agonizing weeks went by, and she didn't hear anything until one evening Tony showed up at her door. She was watching TV and heard the doorbell. When she saw him, she gave out a scream of joy, and they hugged tightly for a while before they could speak. Olivia had tears in her eyes. They sat on the couch in front of the TV.

"Tony, I was so worried," Olivia said. "These last two weeks have been torture. How did you get malaria? Have you recovered? You look so thin!"

After reassuring her that he was well, he explained that he'd been on foot a lot and had probably caught malaria walking through the mangroves. The farmers—guajiros—had helped him with some homemade remedies, but he was very sick and had to be admitted to an army hospital when he returned to US soil. Then he changed topics and started asking about her trip to New York. Gypsy came to smell him wagging her tail, while Olivia and Tony sat snuggled on the couch in front of the TV. Tony fell asleep and awakened to TV static before leaving.

Olivia remained happy because Tony came to see her almost every day. Gypsy would sit on their laps while they watched TV. On weekends, they went to the movies with friends or to the Big Wheel Drive In on Coral Way and 32nd Avenue. The drive-in served its famous Mighty Mo Burger, Tony's favorite. Olivia always made sure to bring something back for Mari.

***

We got news that my Aunt Elena and my cousins were finally leaving Cuba. We had been concerned it would never happen.

Rumors swirled about flights to and from Cuba being suspended, especially after Fidel's declaration and the severing of diplomatic relations.

My father picked them up from the airport and brought them to our house. Elenita was a young lady already, and Pablo was tall. They were all very thin. We stayed up until late that night listening to my aunt's stories about the scarcity of food. They had to use ration cards to get food, and they received only small amounts of meat. For the month, they received one whole chicken, two pounds of rice, two pounds of flour, one pound of sugar, and a dozen eggs. Everything else, even sugar, had to be bought at the black market, which meant risking arrest. We made them hot chocolate with marshmallows that night, and Elenita and I slept together. I was so excited about their arrival that I could hardly fall asleep.

Days later, I went with my father and Aunt Elena to the Freedom Tower. They received a bag of food that included one large can of peanut butter, one large can of lard to use as cooking oil, powdered eggs, powdered milk, a two-pound package of prepared American cheese, a two-pound package of flour, and two large cans of Spam. My father then took his sister to the Holsum Bakery factory on Dixie Highway and 57th Avenue, where they sold day-old loaves for pennies. We always bought our bread there and stored it in the refrigerator so the ants couldn't get to it.

When we got home, my aunt made me a sandwich of fried Spam with American cheese. I didn't care for the Spam. It reminded me of Gypsy's canned dog food. Lucky for us, my aunt made more than Spam during her stay. She would cook dinner, which gave my mother a much-needed break, and from then on, we ate huge Cuban meals, desserts and all.

Not long after, we received news that Manuel, one of my father's cousins and a former Cuban senator, was deathly ill and in the hospital. Olivia and I went with my father to see him. Manuel was my father's favorite cousin and my favorite uncle, and we were close to his family. When we arrived at the hospital, Tía Isa was crying in the waiting room. The doctor had just delivered bad news from the operating room. They told her it could be a virus, and that he had also suffered a stroke. A couple of days later he passed away. The doctors were puzzled; he was fine one day and then dead within the week. Our entire family was devastated. He became the first family member not buried in Cuba, and that pained my father profoundly. "We have to take him back to Cuba when we go back," my father said, "so he can be buried with the rest of the family. We can't leave him behind. Who ever heard of dying from a virus? In Cuba, nobody dies from a virus."

***

A couple of weekends after Tío Manuel's death, Elenita, Pablo, and I got into Tony's car, and he drove us to the Tropicaire Drive-In Theatre. Tony and Olivia took the front seats while the rest of us sat in the back. After we parked, he opened the convertible roof, and we watched *El Cid* under a star-studded February sky. We wrapped ourselves in blankets and ate popcorn while taking in the three-hour movie and forgetting our problems. Afterwards, Tony took us to Hot Shoppes and splurged for milkshakes, which capped a perfect night.

On the way home, with the top still down, we sang along to "Mama Said There'd Be Days Like This" by the Shirelles and then finished the ride singing Frankie Valli's "Can't Take My Eyes Off You." I closed my eyes and asked God for more days like this— carefree, filled with music, and with Olivia by my side. We all thanked Tony repeatedly and hugged him until he couldn't take it anymore.

When we walked into the house, my mother was sitting in front of the TV, fast asleep with the crossword puzzle on her lap. Her books were scattered all around her, and her eyeglasses sat unevenly on her face, one side twisted up to her forehead. Gypsy had fallen asleep on the floor by her feet. I sat next to my mother while my cousins went to sleep in their bunk beds; Elenita was starting a new job and needed to go to training the next day. Olivia was outside saying goodbye to Tony.

"Mami, go to bed, it's late," I whispered in her ear, but she couldn't hear me.

I sat there watching her for a while. She was wearing the white, crochet-knit shawl that she had brought from Cuba. Somehow, it had survived the looting. She kept it in the arm of the couch and would put it on every time she read, did crossword puzzles, or watched TV. Her ivory-white complexion made her seem fragile. But there was nothing fragile about this woman. She was a lion and as determined as an ant at work. Unstoppable. Since she had arrived from Cuba, she had never complained about anything. She went quietly about her duties as a first-grade teacher, came home to study, and took care of her family's supper. Sometimes she could hardly eat, she was so tired. After dinner, she made herself strong Cuban coffee, so she could stay awake and study some more. Always wanting to excel, she needed to study to feed her psyche. She took a variety of courses and exams to obtain more degrees.

On weekends, she treated herself to hours of doing the crossword puzzles she had saved all week from the *Miami Herald*. She treasured the time. Before she came from Cuba, we hadn't had the newspaper delivered. That changed as soon as she got here, and early every morning, the *Miami Herald* appeared at our front door. She read the entire thing every day. Afterwards, she would fold the pages of the crossword puzzle neatly and make a small stack to enjoy on Friday and Saturday nights, when my dad worked late at Pizza Palace.

Mami stirred in her seat and opened her eyes.

"When did you get here?" she asked.

"Just now," I answered.

Then I put my arm over her shoulder and leaned in to hug her. How I wished she would reciprocate, but she didn't. All I could do was hope that she felt for me all the love and pride I felt for her. She had hurt me a lot in the past, but since her arrival in Miami, we seemed to get along better. I appreciated how she tried to make a future for us and make us feel safe. That was how she showed her love.

She got up from the couch, and I helped her pick up the books and newspaper sheets. Gypsy also left the sofa and went to the pillow on the floor, which was her bed.

"Don't forget to lock up before you go to bed," she told me.

"Goodnight, Mami."

She mumbled something that resembled a good night. We were both sleepy.

12

THE RING

Olivia sat up in her bed at the sound of the alarm. She needed to shower and dress nicely. It was finally Valentine's Day. She was sure that Tony would be waiting for her when she got home that afternoon, and she wanted to look pretty for him. This would be their first Valentine's Day together, and she had been dreaming about it for a while. *I hope he likes the sweater I got him,* she thought while she showered. She had wrapped it the night before with some Hershey's kisses inside. She had also made him a handmade greeting card and sealed the envelope with a lipstick kiss.

She hardly ate breakfast and just took a couple of sips of coffee. Before leaving, she stopped by the bathroom one last time to see herself in the mirror. Her medium blonde hair was curled slightly upward in a flip, just the way Tony liked it.

The sun shined in her face when she opened the front door. Once her eyes adjusted, she saw something flying. Squinting to get a better look, she soon realized they were balloons—a dozen or more and in every color. Then she saw the string and the person holding them. It was Tony! She raced to him and kissed him all over while he laughed.

"Take it easy," he said. "They'll fly away!"

"I've been dreaming of our first Valentine's Day, but I never expected this!"

Tony handed the balloons to Olivia and went to the car. He came back with a big heart-shaped box of Schrafft's chocolate candy.

"It's so big, thank you!" Olivia hugged him again. "I'm going back inside to leave these. I can't let them sit in my car."

Olivia came back out with a wrapped present and her card.

"This is yours," she said. "I was going to give it to you later, but it's best you open it now."

Tony delicately removed the wrapping paper and set the box on the hood of his car. He read the card first, then opened the box. Inside was a beautiful, beige shawl-collar cardigan made of a chunky, bulky knit. When he brought it out, the Hershey's kisses fell to the ground. They both laughed and picked them up.

"This is the nicest sweater I've ever had," he told her.

"When you wear it, wherever you are, I want you to think it's me hugging you," Olivia told him while she rubbed her arms.

Tony opened one of the kisses and gave it to Olivia. "I want to take you out to dinner tonight. I already made reservations at a restaurant in Key Biscayne."

"How exciting!" she said. "I'll let my mother know when she gets home from school, but I'm sure she'll say yes."

"I'll pick you up at 6:30 then," he said as he walked to his car.

Olivia started for school. With all the excitement she forgot to mention she had planned to cook for him that night. Maybe she could get a hold of him later.

She called him as soon as she got home that afternoon. Olivia told him about her plan to cook for him that night and save money, but Tony refused the idea.

"I have it all planned," he said, gently. "See you at 6:30."

She still needed to ask her mom, who wasn't home from work yet. Enriqueta would always let Olivia go on double-dates or go alone on short drives to get ice cream, but she had never asked to go on a date like this before. She hoped for the best as she went into her room to pick out a dress.

Just then, Enriqueta walked through the door. Olivia explained that Tony had planned a special date, and Enriqueta granted permission: "Only because it's Valentine's Day, so don't get used to it. And don't be home too late."

Olivia kissed her and hurried into the shower. She didn't have much time, but she went all out with her hair, makeup, jewelry, and her best dress.

The doorbell rang 15 minutes early. Olivia could hear Mari and Enriqueta carrying on a conversation with Tony while she finished up. She finally sprayed on her favorite perfume, L'Air du Temps, which Tony loved.

Tony stood when Olivia walked into the family room. He told her he had never seen her look so beautiful. He was wearing her gift over a dress shirt and tie. Olivia thought he was the handsomest guy on earth.

"Look what Tony brought me, Olivia."

Mari was holding a smaller version of her own box of chocolates, her eyes wide with joy.

"Thank you, Tony," Olivia said, touched by his thoughtfulness. "That's so sweet of you." Enriqueta came closer to Mari, and she thanked Tony affectionately.

He turned to Olivia. "We need to go. We have reservations at the restaurant."

As he opened her door, Olivia couldn't help but notice that he was a bit nervous. Her heart sank as she wondered if had received news of a new mission.

"Are you ok, Tony?"

"Yes, why do you ask?"

"I'm probably imagining things," she said quietly.

"It's just a long drive, and I don't want to miss our reservations. It's a busy night for restaurants, and I don't want to lose our table to someone else."

As they drove on the Rickenbacker Causeway to Key Biscayne, they could see the Atlantic on their right and part of the Miami skyline on their left. The view was spectacular, as the last rays of the sun fought to stay alive. The windows were rolled down, and she took a deep breath to inhale the smell of the ocean.

Tony suddenly asked, "Are you happy?"

"Very much so," she said. "How about you?"

"Couldn't be any happier," Tony said with a big smile.

They arrived at the Jamaica Inn in time for their reservation. It was one of Miami's finest restaurants. Olivia had heard of it but was surprised to be there.

The host escorted them to a table. When the server came, Tony ordered the prime rib for himself and the fried shrimp for Olivia. She quickly fell in love with the chef's secret batter, and they ate while looking into each other's eyes.

They ordered chocolate-covered strawberries for dessert, and Tony excused himself to go to the restroom. He still seemed a bit nervous. Olivia planned to ask him about it before the night was over, but she didn't want to spoil the beautiful meal.

Tony finally came back just as the chocolate-covered strawberries arrived. The server laid down six strawberries, and Tony placed three strawberries on each of their plates. Olivia thanked him and grabbed the first strawberry. It was juicy and delicious. She thought of her aunts and uncles who had taken jobs picking strawberries in Homestead. It was grueling work, but it was all they could get after arriving in Miami from Cuba.

Just when Olivia reached for a second strawberry, something caught her eye. It looked like ice. When she looked closer, she saw a ring inside it.

She froze. Her hands and feet turned cold. What was this? Smiling, Tony grabbed the strawberry from her hand and held the ring delicately, looking up into Olivia's eyes. Olivia's mouth was wide open, and she was starting to cry. Tony grabbed her hand and squeezed it.

"Olivia, will you marry me?" His expression was solemn.

Tears kept her from speaking. A million things flashed through her mind. What did it mean? They were both young, and she still had three months of school before graduation. Was he ready to settle down and get married? But she loved him immensely.

"Yes!" she said quickly, so that she couldn't change her mind.

The surrounding tables applauded, and a couple of waiters came to congratulate them. Tony was still fumbling with the ring and finally slid it on.

"Mari helped me with the ring sizing," he said. "She brought me one of your rings and I took it to the jewelers."

"Oh, so Mari was in on it?" Olivia laughed.

The ring was beautiful and simple—a sparkling square-cut solitaire diamond with a good, colorless shine and set in white gold. Not too big and not too small. Olivia couldn't stop looking at it.

"But Tony, what does it mean? Are you quitting the CIA? When do you want to get married?"

"It means we're *engaged*," he said. "We have plenty of time to get married." He explained that they were close to a breakthrough at work. "Whatever happens, I hope to be done with it by Christmas time, so we can get married soon."

Olivia's head was spinning. She could be married by this time next year.

They left the restaurant filled with love and joy. They kissed and hugged passionately in the car but went no further. Olivia had told Tony in the beginning of their relationship that they would wait until they were married, and Tony respected that. They parked their car beside the Rickenbacker bridge, next to the shores of the Atlantic Ocean. They talked about their future and about how many kids they wanted. They made all the promises that their love could hold. Then Tony turned on the radio and held out his hand to her, and they slow-danced in the sand for what seemed like hours.

He brought her home close to midnight. Mari was awake in her bed waiting for Olivia.

"Let me see the ring!" she yelled out as soon as Olivia entered the house.

Olivia showed her proudly and whirled with joy.

"Tony was so nervous, Mari. I thought something else was wrong with him."

"Olivia, I've never seen such a beautiful ring!"

They talked for a while until their eyes got heavy.

"We have school tomorrow," said Olivia. "So let's go to sleep."

"Olivia, is Tony going to stop traveling now? Will he get a different job?"

"I don't know, Mari. I hope he does, but at this point, I love him so much, it doesn't matter. I can't do anything about his job. All I can do is support him and give him love and peace."

"Olivia?"

"Yes, Mari?"

"You remind me of the ducks."

"Oh, Mari. You and your duck fascination. What do you mean by that?"

"They look so peaceful," Mari said, "poised and serene in the water, but the whole time they're paddling and struggling to keep afloat."

"Mari, you say the funniest things!" Olivia laughed.

"No one in this world has a sister like you, Olivia."

"I can say the same thing about you, Mari."

∗∗∗

Mari lay awake thinking about her sister. How long could Olivia keep this up? She knew how Olivia cried at night but never complained. All she gave Tony were smiles and love. She thought of Pablo Neruda's *100 Love Sonnets*. She was reading it in secret because her father said Neruda was a communist and forbade her from reading his work. Neruda spoke of loving in a deep way: "in secret, between the shadow and the soul." Olivia's love was just as deep, but so was her struggle.

Mari wondered if one day she would meet a boy, or a man, that she could love as much. *It must be nice*, she thought, *to care about someone so much that you want to spend your whole life with them.* She was sure that she could never love as selflessly as Olivia could. Watching Olivia suffer so much made Mari glad she wasn't in love. *Did it have to bring so much pain?* she wondered.

13

Liebestraum (Love Dream)

The rest of the week went by slowly for Olivia. Her mind was on Tony and her engagement ring. Sitting in a classroom all day and worrying about schoolwork seemed like a waste when she knew she would be married soon. She couldn't focus on her studies when longing for Tony, and the thought of being his wife consumed her.

On Friday afternoon, she hurried home from school because Tony had told her they were going to the drive-in with his friend Humberto and his girlfriend. She also looked forward to Saturday, when she would go to the conservatory to meet the director. Tony had insisted she go, and she knew that studying piano would fill her days, and her mind, when he was "on the road again," as Mari would say.

When she walked into the house, the phone was ringing. She raced to get it.

"Olivia, I've been calling you," Tony said with urgency.

"I just got in, my love," Olivia said. "What's that noise in the background? Are you on the street?"

"We won't be able to go to the movies tonight," he said, breathless. "I've already called Humberto to cancel."

"Will I see you later tonight?" Olivia asked, already knowing the answer.

"No, you won't," he said. "Try to go to the movies with Mari tonight. Don't stay home."

"I will wait until we see that movie together."

"Whatever you want," he said and paused. "Love you, Olivia. See you later." He hung up.

She was beginning to hate those three words. Why couldn't he say *see you tomorrow, see you in a few hours,* or *see you Monday?*

Olivia went quickly into her room and threw herself on the bed. She cried into her pillow. She knew that he was leaving, but not when he would return. "Please let him be safe," she prayed to God. "Let him come back to me soon." She cried and prayed herself to sleep.

The next morning, Olivia woke up to Enriqueta's voice. "Olivia, get up. We need to be in the conservatory at 11 this morning."

"No, Mami, I don't want to go."

"What do you mean?" Enriqueta said. "We confirmed two days ago, and the director is waiting to meet you today. What happened?

The tears started to come, so she turned away from Enriqueta to hide them. "Tony left again yesterday, and I have a headache."

"I knew something was wrong when Mari told me you went to sleep early. He needed to work, *mijita.* It's hard for him to be on the road like that. If you are going to marry him, you must support him and keep busy. He told me he wanted you to resume your piano lessons."

"When did he tell you that, Mami?"

"The other day when he was sitting on the couch with me. He told me that he was going to do a lot of traveling because they had expanded his territory, and he was worried about you being alone for long periods of time. He thought that resuming your piano would be fulfilling and would keep your mind busy. He also said that there was nothing that would make him happier than to see you start playing again."

Olivia turned to look at her mother. "Did he really say that, Mami?"

"Of course, *mijita*. I wouldn't make up something like that."

Olivia checked the clock on her nightstand. It was 9 a.m. She could get up and take a shower to see if she felt better. She needed to do something today or she would go crazy with worry. Keeping Tony's secret made her chest tighten.

She went through the motions of getting ready, and after a quick breakfast, Olivia and Enriqueta left for the conservatory on Coral Way. Called the Music Studio, it was owned by a French couple— she was an opera singer, and he a world-renowned pianist. As soon as she walked in, Olivia felt at home. She could hear the sounds of the Czerny piano scales as well as voice exercises from the lobby. The receptionist told Olivia and Enriqueta to take a seat while the director finished a call. The door behind the reception area opened, and Fabien Lambert came out. He was well into his sixties and looked handsome with his salt-and-pepper hair. He spoke good English with only a slight French accent. He led them to his office and then got right to the point.

"Olivia, your mother has told me all about you and your piano talent," he said. "She also mentioned that you don't have a piano to practice on and that you haven't practiced in over two years. What is the last piece you were working at before you left Cuba?"

"Liszt, 'Liebestraum No. 3,'" Olivia answered in a shaky voice, "and I performed Rachmaninoff's 'The Bells of Moscow,' Prelude in C# Minor, in an international competition."

"Did you win anything?" he asked.

"First place," she said, shyly.

"Would you mind playing one or both of them for me?"

Olivia felt her heart drop. "I don't know if I can. I haven't played at all for so long."

"I know you will make errors," he said. "I just want to get a feel for your musicality and technique."

Olivia gave Enriqueta a pleading look, but Enriqueta did not give in. "You'll be fine. Just play what you remember."

Fabien led Olivia to a classroom with a stunning grand piano. Olivia's legs were shaking, and her hands felt cold. But the beauty of the piano mesmerized her. She sat and ran her fingers over the keys without pressing them. Immediately, she felt the warmth of the instrument, and her heartbeat slowed down. Her senses awakened as she started playing Liszt's "Liebestraum." She played the piece beautifully and with emotion, as Fabien stood silently watching her. When Olivia finished, she had tears in her eyes.

"I didn't forget," she said.

Fabien sat next to her on the bench. "When can you start?"

A half an hour later, Enriqueta and Olivia left the conservatory with a folder full of papers. They included a copy of the scholarship, a set of the conservatory's rules, and a list of recitals and competitions with corresponding dates. Monsieur Lambert had assured them he would help find a used piano for Olivia. He wanted to see her twice a week, right after school.

As she drove home, Olivia thought of Tony. She wished she could call him and tell him all about the experience. Maybe one day she could play for Tony, she thought. She smiled the whole way home.

That night, she thought of the possibilities, of how the future held new happiness for her. She also thought about their wedding day. He would be home soon, and she had so much to tell him.

***

Tony rested along the banks of *El Río Cauto* in Santiago de Cuba, sitting with his guide and helper and sharing water. They were on their way to Manzanillo to deliver weapons to a group of guajiros and were traveling at night to avoid detection. They arrived at their destination before dawn and gathered a couple of the farmers to help bury the combat rifles in steel barrels. After the work was finished, Tony found a cave and pulled out his telegraph to report success. He planned to stay in the Manzanillo area for a few days organizing cells in the area before heading to the pickup point. For now, he needed sleep. He had been walking for 10 hours straight carrying a heavy load. The next morning, he would get something to eat and then start his rounds. The ground beneath him was hard and unforgiving, but his exhaustion won out, and he was asleep in minutes.

***

Olivia had trouble getting out of bed for school. She now saw it as a burden and went through her school days in a trance. She thought only about marrying Tony. Everything else was unimportant. She was looking forward to piano though, especially after seeing that beautiful grand piano. She loved the feel of the keys.

She was reminded of the piano when she answered Fabien Lambert's call asking for Enriqueta.

"She's not home from work yet, Mr. Lambert," Olivia said.

"Please have her call me when she gets back."

Olivia wondered why he had called but couldn't think of a reason.

She got her answer when Eniqueta returned from work and called him back. Enriqueta told Olivia the news as soon as she hung up. Monsieur Lambert had found a used piano that one of his teachers was selling.

"But Mami," said Olivia, "we can't afford this right now."

"It won't hurt to go see it," her mother said. "I'm going to lie down and rest a bit, and then we will go."

Fabien had given Enriqueta the piano teacher's address, and she and Olivia went there that evening. The teacher, Louise, led them to a brown, upright piano that had been in her family for more than 30 years. Louise wasn't using it because she had bought a grand piano recently.

Olivia walked to the piano and slid her fingers over the cover.

"You can open it and play it if you want," said Louise, "but I'm sure it needs tuning."

The piano felt good to the touch but did need tuning. After Olivia played briefly, Enriqueta started talking to Louise about the price and other details. Olivia sat on the bench, looking out on a big backyard with a huge avocado tree. It made her think of Tony and his stories of eating figs, mangos, and avocados he had plucked out of trees. She wondered where he was at that moment, but just as her mind drifted, Enriqueta called her name and said it was time to leave.

On the way home, Enriqueta delivered the news: "The piano is out of our reach for now; we will find something that's not so expensive."

"Don't worry, Mami. I'm going twice a week to the conservatory, and I think I can also find a room to practice after class. I'll ask Monsieur Lambert."

When they pulled up to the house, Elena was waiting for them on the porch. She had locked herself out of their garage apartment.

"Don't cook today, Enriqueta," Elena said. "I'm going to make lentils. I will bring them over. I need to speak to you anyway."

***

Aunt Elena made a delicious dinner for us that included lentils with Spanish sausage, ham, carrots, and potatoes. Then she gave us the news that she and her kids were moving out. Elenita had been working a new job at the hospital, but it was far from the house. She had to take three buses each way and got home late at night. Pablo was now working with her, and they had found a small apartment within walking distance. With Aunt Elena's sewing money, they felt they could afford it.

Aunt Elena said, "I will speak with Lorenzo tomorrow and get his opinion, but I wanted to make sure that I told you tonight. I'm very grateful for all your help." She hugged Enriqueta, Olivia, and me. We were all sad and knew we would miss them, but the garage wouldn't stay empty for long. Another aunt was coming with her husband and their four children. At least the timing had worked out.

Around the time Aunt Elena and her family moved out, Olivia started spending more time at the conservatory. She learned from a teacher named Gloria, a concert pianist who had taught at the conservatory for many years. Gloria taught Olivia on Tuesdays and Thursdays and then let her use the back classroom for practice. Not only was Olivia gone those evenings, but she also added Friday evenings to her work schedule. She was saving for a piano. To help her with money, Mari asked her boss for two more weekday evenings. She also took on more babysitting jobs and even raised her rate. She wanted her sister to have the piano as soon as possible, but she kept it a secret.

14

The Competition

It was March, and Olivia had not heard from Tony in more than three weeks. Only her piano lessons and work kept her sane. Sitting in school all day became agony, and she struggled to maintain good grades. She was counting down the days until the year ended.

She had become curious about a piano competition that Gloria mentioned called the Cliburn, which was to take place in Texas over the summer. Mr. Lambert would select a handful of students of different ages to compete. Olivia thought of her performance in Mexico, where she had won first prize, but that seemed like a lifetime ago.

In the afternoons, Olivia took turns with Mari walking Gypsy. Everyone in the family loved and doted on Gypsy, even Lorenzo. She would wag her tail every time she saw him. Olivia was just leaving to walk her when Mari returned from school.

"Let's walk her together," Olivia said to Mari.

They started walking, and Mari asked a question: "Olivia, can you give me a ride to the drug store tonight? My boss wants me to come in earlier. He is doing inventory."

"Of course, Mari, and I can also pick you up."

At the next piano lesson, Olivia was called into Monsieur Lambert's office. He told her that he wanted her to get ready to compete in the Cliburn Competition this summer.

"Monsieur Lambert, I don't think I'm ready for that."

"Probably not, but you will be by June," he said confidently.

"What would I play?"

"You have to play a mandatory étude and another piece in the first round. You can repeat anything in your repertoire in the final. I will choose strong pieces."

"Is anyone else from the conservatory competing?" Olivia asked before she left.

"Only one other student, Vivian Chui."

Olivia left the conservatory with an uneasy feeling. She would have rather been given the opportunity to decide for herself, especially when it came to the repertoire. The whole thing made her uncomfortable. She confronted her mother with her concerns as soon as she got home.

"Olivia, you have a scholarship," said Enriqueta, "so he expects you to represent the conservatory in competitions."

"But why, Mami? Are you sure about this?"

Enriqueta pulled out the scholarship papers and read aloud from them: "Students must participate and perform in all activities assigned by the conservatory. This includes recitals, music competitions, ensembles, and fairs."

"It makes me uncomfortable."

"I don't understand why, Olivia. You used to love competitions."

"He thinks I'm better than I am," Olivia lamented. "I'm sure he will pick something hard."

Olivia learned about her pieces at her next class. For the required pieces, she had to choose two of the Bach French Suites of the Baroque era. For her own selections, Mr. Lambert picked Brahms's "Intermezzo in A," Op. 118 from the Romantic era for the first round, Liszt's "Liebestraum" and Rachmaninoff's "The Bells of Moscow" for the second, and Chopin's Étude in E Major,

"Tristesse," for the finals.

She returned home agitated. "This man is crazy, Mami. He wants me to learn two brand new, impossible pieces, and the competition is only three months away! Then he tells me I can practice at the conservatory every afternoon because someone is always there."

"Olivia, all I can tell you is that he must think you can do it!"

"But why me, Mami? There are other great students there."

She threw her hands up and went to her room. Enriqueta followed her.

"Please, go away," Olivia said. "I want to be alone."

Enriqueta respected her wishes. Olivia wept, not only about the competition but about the emptiness she felt when Tony was away. She also worried about the danger he could be in. The pressure was too much.

When Enriqueta left the room, Mari approached her. "Here, Mami. This is for Olivia's piano." She handed her the bills she had just counted. It totaled $28.

Enriqueta looked stunned. She thanked Mari and went right to the telephone table and dialed Louise's number. She told Louise about the competition, and asked Louise if she would accept payment in installments of $50 per month.

A few days later, two men delivered the piano.

That same afternoon, as Olivia walked to her car at the school parking lot, she saw Tony leaning on her car. She ran as fast as her book load allowed and dropped everything to hug him.

"Tony, these have been the longest three weeks of my life. What took you so long?"

"It was long for me too, but I'm back now."

She saw that he limped as he walked to the car door. He had also lost weight.

"Why are you limping?" Olivia asked.

Tony motioned for her to get in the car so they could talk. He sat down uneasily and then explained that he'd been shot in the leg while running from Castro's militia. He had hidden in a cave for two days. "Fortunately, the guajiros brought me some food. One of the farmers I was working with was shot, and his family was arrested. He died before they could interrogate him, otherwise he would have exposed the entire operation." Tony explained that he missed the pickup, but that agents came back for him and eventually brought him to a military hospital. He had to stay a while because his wound was infected.

"Why didn't you let me know?" Olivia asked.

"Olivia, you know I can't call," he said, agitated. "I can't explain these things over a phone line."

Olivia covered her face and started to sob. Tony hugged her tightly.

"Don't worry, I'm here now," he said. "I will always come back to you."

"Why were you in a cave instead of a safe house?"

"Please don't ask any more questions."

"You could get killed, and I wouldn't even know."

"I don't know what to tell you. I need to get my father out of jail. And I need you to be brave."

She opened the car door and got out to catch her breath. After she calmed down, they went across the street to a place that made fresh fruit juice. Tony bought her a mango-orange juice, her favorite. A couple of hours later, they started for home in their cars.

Olivia walked into the house and saw Enriqueta sitting on a piano bench. Then she saw the piano.

"Mami, what have you done? How can you afford this?"

"Don't worry about that, Olivia," said Enriqueta, brushing her hand across the keys. "With this, you'll be able to practice at home." Enriqueta explained that someone would be coming tomorrow to tune it.

Olivia thanked her profusely. *Happy surprises come in bunches,* she thought, *just like painful ones.*

Enriqueta looked over Olivia's shoulder and saw Tony. "Welcome back, stranger," she said, pleased as he came to greet her. "When did you get back, and why are you limping?"

"I twisted my ankle when I was out jogging," he replied.

Enriqueta invited him to stay for dinner. She had just made a delicious Spanish cod fish stew, *Bacalao a la Vizcaina*. He obliged and ate two helpings.

"It's been a while since I've had a home-cooked meal," Tony said.

"You were on the road for a while this time," Enriqueta said. "It looks like you've lost weight."

Olivia acted quickly. "Have you visited your mother yet?" she asked.

"I called her and said I would drop by after I left here tonight," he answered. "I'll have dinner with her tomorrow."

After an hour of eating and visiting, Tony excused himself. "I better get going. I need to catch up on my sleep."

When Tony left, Olivia sat down at the piano and played for hours, until her eyes were heavy. Playing the piano was like therapy. It relaxed her emotions and her body. Her mind emptied of all negative thoughts and welcomed the soothing effect of the music. She stood up after she tired. *I hope Mami knows how much I appreciate this piano.* Tomorrow, she would thank Enriqueta properly. She prayed intensely that night. *Please God, don't let Tony go back to Cuba. Don't take him from me.* She couldn't wait until tomorrow, when she would have Tony all to herself and they could talk. Sleep came to her fast that night.

Tony and Olivia went on a picnic at Matheson Hammock Bay that Saturday. There, he gave her the news. He planned to resign from the agency but only after following through on an important assignment.

"I'll tell them I can only work until Christmas," he said. "Then we can get married and start a new life together. I'll try to open a business with the money I've saved."

"Can't you just quit right now?" she asked. "You've already been wounded."

"Please don't ask me for that," he said. "There's a lot going on you don't know about. I need to see it through." She looked disappointed. He told her they should focus on wedding plans, but it failed to lift her spirits. Rather than distract her, he tried to assure her one last time about his remaining assignments. "Trust me," he said, "I will always come back."

She started to feel at ease, but then a thought occurred to her. "Tony, what about your mother and brother? Do they know about us? That we're getting married?"

"I avoid talking to my mother because she asks a lot of questions. If she sits down with your mother, she'll ask even more. She must suspect something about my job because I give her money every month and she knows that selling encyclopedias wouldn't allow for that."

Olivia understood and nodded.

"Let's try to wait a while longer before we tell her," he said. It sounded logical, but it was easier said than done.

"Ok, but I need to tell my mother," she said. "We have to plan a wedding, and I have to get my wedding dress."

They agreed to have the families meet at a later date and that Olivia and her mother should start planning the wedding.

"Tony," Olivia asked, shyly, "I am entering a piano competition in June. It's in Texas. Will you be able to come with me?"

"Let me know the dates, my love. I'll try."

Riding back home with the convertible top down, Olivia felt invigorated and happy. Everything was coming together, almost like a dream. All she needed was for Tony to be safe. She turned to look directly at him as he drove.

"Tony, you need to take care of yourself," she said. "You need to stay safe on these missions."

His smile disappeared. "Olivia, what kind of request is that? It's not in my power. We all risk our lives when we go out into the world every day. Do you think I'm reckless? All I think of is coming back to you. So please don't think about my safety. Just know that every time I leave, my heart is here with you."

Later that night, Olivia sat down with Enriqueta and told her the news. Having received permission from Tony beforehand, she also gave her mother a vague notion of Tony's activities without mentioning the CIA or spying. Enriqueta could only know that Tony was training in an undisclosed location in preparation for another invasion. This was as much as Tony's mother knew, which would make things easier when the two would finally meet.

Enriqueta was not surprised by the news. "I knew these absences and the silence meant he was somewhere incommunicado. I just didn't want to make things harder on you by probing."

"Thank you, Mami."

"I'm guessing he belongs to the Cuban Democratic Youth, right?"

Olivia didn't answer. Enriqueta continued cynically. "The Cuban youth have not learned their lesson. Didn't we lose enough men to the Bay of Pigs invasion?" Enriqueta stopped herself momentarily and rubbed her temples. "Oh Olivia, no wonder you have been so unhappy. Why didn't you tell us before?"

Olivia shrugged. Her mother understood that she couldn't answer, so Enriqueta changed the subject and started talking about a wedding dress. "Your Tía Eulalia is a great seamstress," she said. "I have seen the long evening gowns that she makes for your cousins, and she has impeccable taste."

Olivia felt relief. Her mother was taking charge of important wedding arrangements, and Olivia knew Enriqueta would leave nothing to chance. This help would allow Olivia to devote more time to the competition.

***

As always, when Tony was in Miami, he came by every day. Olivia cut back her work hours to spend more time with him and to practice for the competition. He came over almost every evening and stayed late. She would only start practicing after he left, which meant less sleep. Fortunately for Olivia, Easter arrived, and a week's vacation followed. During this time, she played all day, every day. My mother and I would sit and listen for hours as her performance of those three pieces began to take shape.

May came around and so did graduation. Olivia had counted down the days. Immediate family and some friends attended the ceremony, and we ended up at Sambo's on Coral Way for dinner. I had their delicious pancakes, but Olivia hardly ate. She was nervous because the competition was only three weeks away.

After graduation, she practiced nonstop. Monsieur Lambert was worried about her tempo. "You're not in control of the piece," he kept telling her. He made her go back to using a metronome, which she had stopped using months before. During one session, as the metronome ticked away, I overheard my mother talking on the phone making travel plans for the competition. She mentioned that she would be traveling with Olivia, and that Lucia, who had saved money for the airfare, was also going.

"Will I be going, too?" I asked.

"You are staying here with your father," she said. "The conservatory is buying Olivia's airfare, but I must pay my own way. We are short on money, especially now that we need to save for the wedding."

I was heartbroken. The possibility of not attending had never occurred to me. I excused myself and went to my room and cried. In the days that followed, I tried to hide my emotions, because I didn't want to distract Olivia. She had enough to worry about. She played nearly every waking hour, and Tony kept his visits short.

During one of his last visits before the competition, he got my attention and handed me an envelope. "Your sister was sad you couldn't come. Now you can."

I looked inside the envelope and saw the ticket.

"Tony, I can't accept this," I said, breathless. "It costs too much money!"

"Take it. No arguments. I already told your mother, and we're good."

My heart raced with joy, and I hugged him. "Thank you, Tony. You're the best!"

We arrived in Dallas early on Friday, Olivia's birthday, and went straight to Fort Worth. Our motel was within walking distance to Texas Christian University, where the competition was to take place. Olivia had asked us not to remind her of her birthday until the competition was over. The preliminary rounds would happen on Saturday morning and the semifinals that night. The finals would take place on Sunday afternoon, and the winners would be announced afterwards.

At the hotel, Tony had his own room, a single, while the rest of us stayed in a double. Our room was ample, with two double beds and a wall air-conditioning unit. Lucia had not arrived yet because her flight was due later. Olivia sat on one of the beds and stayed quiet and focused. In the afternoon, she left for the university with Mr. and Mrs. Lambert to find a room to practice in, coming back a few hours later with pizza for us all. Lucia had finally arrived, and she handed Olivia a present.

"Happy birthday, Olivia!" Lucia said happily.

Olivia put the boxes of pizza on the small table in the room, and they hugged.

"Luci, if you don't mind, I'll open my present on Sunday after the competition is over."

"It's OK, I understand. We will wait."

Olivia got Tony, and we all sat with pizza and napkins, laughing. We tried to lighten the mood, but Olivia was tense.

"Guys, I need to get to bed early," she said. "You can go to Tony's room with the pizza if you want."

Lucia and I brought the pizza to Tony's room while my mother stayed behind, and Tony and Olivia stepped into the hallway to say goodnight. I kept Tony's door propped open.

"Do you know that I am the youngest player in my category?" I overheard Olivia ask. "There's a young Russian who is also 19, but he will be 20 next month. I just turned 19 today."

"Age doesn't matter, my love. It's your passion and your connection with the piano that will set you apart from all of them."

"Tony, I know I can't win this competition," Olivia said. "There are only four American pianists and one from Italy. The other 15 are Soviet, Asian, or German, and they practice all day in those countries. They go to special schools for competitions like this. I feel so bad that you've all come down here to see me lose."

"Stop right there," Tony said, emphatically. "Nothing could have kept me from being here. We're here because we love you."

He was right. He had managed to calm her down, and they said goodnight. He came back to the room, and I quickly moved away from the door and sat on the bed. Tony, Luci, and I finished eating our pizza and watched some TV before saying good night.

The preliminary round started at 9 a.m. It was held behind closed doors and took most of the day. By 4 p.m. the names of the eight semifinalists were posted outside the auditorium door. Olivia's was one of them! Vivian, the younger contestant from the conservatory, had made the finals in the 12–18 age group. Monsieur Lambert and his wife were thrilled. At 7 p.m., the semifinalists would perform for the judges, again behind closed doors. We were all disappointed that we couldn't see Olivia play. Only the four finalists in each age group would perform on Sunday afternoon in front of a live audience.

Saturday night, we all went to sleep not knowing if Olivia had made the finals. It was Tony who got up early to go check the list. At 8:30 a.m., he knocked on our hotel room door. Olivia opened it, and he handed her a bouquet of red carnations and a card.

"Sorry, these were the only flowers I could find at the Tom Thumb store," he said. "You are one of the finalists, my love!"

"What?" Olivia shouted. "Are you sure?"

"Positive," he said. "Your name is up there with the Russians. Vivian didn't make it, unfortunately. I saw her father there."

I hugged Mami, who was my bedmate, and Luci squealed and bounced on the bed on her knees.

"Quiet down," said Enriqueta. "You're going to wake all the guests."

***

Olivia changed out of her pajamas and went with Tony to have breakfast. She stopped at the front desk of the motel and asked the attendant to ring Mr. Lambert's room. He dialed for Mr. Lambert and handed Olivia the phone.

"Good morning, Monsieur Lambert," she said. "Did you hear the news?"

"Yes, Olivia, it's very exciting. I was going to tell you this morning."

She barely let him finish. "Monsieur Lambert, can I play 'The Bells of Moscow' again for the finals? You told me we could repeat any piece in the finals, and I feel more confident in that one because I've been playing it so long."

"You could also play Chopin's Étude," he said. "You have up to 15 minutes, so that gives you time to play both. Either way, let me know because I have to submit the scores to the judges ahead of time. Meet me at the university in one hour so you can practice and then decide."

Olivia hung up with a sick feeling in her stomach. She loved Chopin's Étude but wasn't confident in how she played it. Also, Tony loved "The Bells of Moscow," and she wanted to surprise him.

They went to a donut shop nearby for a quick breakfast. Afterwards, Tony walked her to the university. She stayed to practice for a few hours, and Tony went back to the motel to make a long-distance call.

That evening, with an audience of more than 100 people and five judges, Olivia played for her family and the love of her life. Six months before, she never could have imagined having this opportunity to play for the people she adored. Olivia mesmerized the audience with her interpretations of the Chopin Étude and Rachmaninoff's "The Bells of Moscow." When she finished, she received a standing ovation. Standing there and bowing, with her heart full of passion, she told herself, *Happy Birthday, Olivia!*

She went backstage to wait for the two remaining contestants and the results of the judges.

Olivia didn't win first prize, nor did she win second. Third prize was fine by her and more than she had expected just a few months before. As she received the award, she felt peace. She had given it her all and had made her mom and Monsieur Lambert proud.

We all went out to celebrate her birthday at an Italian restaurant. Enriqueta was quiet and hardly ate. Nervousness had worn her out.

On the plane ride home, Tony and Olivia held hands. He seemed distracted.

"Are you ok, Tony?" she asked.

"I will be leaving right after we get back," he said. "They are waiting for me."

"When did you find out?"

"They told me last night when I checked in. The mission was delayed for a week because I requested the time."

She looked distraught, and Tony was pressing her hand. "You need to let me go in peace, Olivia."

For the rest of the flight, Olivia kept her eyes closed. When they arrived at the airport, Tony hailed a taxi for the family and said goodbye. Then he hailed his own. Olivia saw it speed past theirs, and tears filled her eyes.

Enriqueta said, "I am so glad that Tony came. He was so proud of you."

"And I am proud of him," Olivia replied.

15

The Crisis

In the middle of the night, Tony and his two men jumped out of the rubber craft and into the water. They swam a short distance with their gear to a small beach located 10 kilometers west of the city of Santiago de Cuba and, after they reached land, made their way to the cave. Two men were waiting there to be relieved, and they looked anxious as they debriefed Tony. They said the guajiros, who had helped the operatives and had brought food occasionally, were now scared and refused to cooperate. A militia had moved into the area, and security was tight. Tony thanked the men for their report, and they left for the pickup point.

Tony and his crew then started their trek through the mountains. Eventually they reached an abandoned copper mine, where they dug for the empty barrels left by the last crew. Once the men reached the barrels, they loaded the weapons they'd brought and reburied the barrels, making sure to level off the soil and cover it with the branches. Exhausted, they returned to the cave before daybreak and slept heavily.

Tony was awakened by thirst, and he looked at his watch. It was almost 5 p.m. They had slept for 12 hours, which now put them behind. They decided to split up. Tony would head to the safe house, while the other two would head out to the farms to seek food from guajiros friendly to the cause.

Tony walked for hours and didn't arrive at the safe house till midnight. As he approached, he could see a light on the porch and someone sitting in a rocking chair, smoking a cigar. It looked like Manuel.

"Antonio is that you?" Manuel whispered.

"Yes," Tony replied.

"Keep your voice down. On the other side of this wall," he said, pointing at the wall that divided the two small houses, "lives a communist family. Their son is a big shot in Castro's government."

Manuel brought Tony up to speed on what was happening. Soldiers and their families had come to the area and were now moving into empty houses that had been confiscated by the government. Manuel asked Tony to wait outside and went into the house. He came back with a big can of water and some bread and *harina* (grits) that Ana had made. Tony stayed hidden under a tree while he devoured the food. Manuel brought him more bread and fruits to take back and then gave him a ride to the jagüey tree, where he promised to leave Tony more food after things calmed down. Tony walked the rest of the way back to the cave.

For the next few days, Tony visited some of the contacts he had established and found them scared and uncooperative. The presence of Castro's military was evident in the remote region. Cargo trucks rumbled throughout the area, which was unusual. A few of the farmers told Tony that the government was installing a new irrigation system in the area. Tony was skeptical but said nothing. That night, he noted the activity in his report. It wasn't safe to use the main roads, so the men stuck to pathways on the sides of the hills to travel between towns. Three days later, he asked for further instructions. He was told only to get ready for pickup. *This is a short one*, he thought. He left with a feeling that things were about to get worse and that he would be back soon.

***

Back home, Tony and Olivia spent the next few weeks planning their future. They went to the church to speak to Father Julian, a close friend of the family, about their wedding. They couldn't commit to a date yet, but Father Julian promised to be flexible. Father Julian was originally from San Sebastian, a city on the northern coast of Spain, and he directed the church choir. Olivia, Lucy, and Mari had been choir members since their arrival from Cuba, and Enriqueta came to confession often. He had become the family's spiritual advisor.

"I'm very happy for you," Father Julian told the couple. "God will let you know when the time is right."

That time would be later rather than sooner. In July, word reached the CIA that Castro had allowed the Soviets to place nuclear missiles in Cuba. On September 4, 1962, President John F. Kennedy issued a warning against the introduction of offensive weapons in Cuba. That night, Tony said goodbye to Olivia and began a new mission.

The objective was clear: find out the location of the missile bases and figure out what kind of missiles, if any, were coming in. To obtain that information, Tony and his crew needed to mix with locals. Manuel brought them clothing and hats from the guajiros and even militia uniforms. They would use horses, wagons, and an old car that Manuel provided to get around the island.

The men started in the west end of Cuba and traveled east. They observed construction activity around different towns and noticed many Russian "visitors." The CIA confirmed that these visitors were military specialists, engineers of missile construction in Russia. They had come to Cuba disguised as agricultural experts. They oversaw the digging of trenches meant not for irrigation but for nuclear missiles. The agents managed to photograph their equipment and their work, which was extensive in the town of San Cristobal in the province of Pinar del Río. In Manzanillo, Oriente, ships delivered large crates labeled as irrigation supplies. President Kennedy's warning had come too late. The plan to install nuclear missiles 90 miles from the US was well underway.

Tony returned home two weeks later, but only for a short time. Olivia was unaware of what was going on inside of Cuba but knew something was unusual. She complained to Tony that he was hiding something from her.

"There is a lot going on that I can't talk about," he said, and reminded her that he had to finish his work before leaving the agency. "I can't leave any loose ends. The quicker I finish, the quicker we can have our wedding."

On his next trip back, he found the island even busier with dubious activity. Trucks passed through town at all hours rather than just at night as before. Tony found the change alarming. Cuba had one main road that served as the artery of the island. Called "Carretera Central," it connected one end of the island to the other and took about 13 hours to drive. The main port of entry for the missiles was Manzanillo Bay in the southeast tip of Cuba. From there, trucks would head for San Cristobal on the northwest coast, the closest point on Cuba to the US. The agency wanted to know what type of nuclear weapons were entering, so Tony and his crew photographed what they saw. They found more sites than the agency had expected and noticed more Soviet personnel than ever. The size and number of wheels on the trucks gave them an idea of how heavy the cargo was, which gave them a clue as to the size of the missiles.

After three weeks of surveillance, Tony and his crew returned to their hideout. They received a communication saying things were heating up and that it was time for the crew to pull out. Tony felt relief. It was October 14, and he had been in Cuba for almost three weeks.

He breathed easier the next day when they made it safely to the mothership. As it headed for the Florida coast, he felt great satisfaction. Perro Negro had been successful, and he was coming back safely to Olivia. He sat on the deck and looked at the stars on that clear night. They looked brighter than ever. In a matter of days, he would put in his request to be placed on the inactive list. Then he could focus on his new life. What he didn't know was that the same day he left the island, a US U-2 spy plane had taken hundreds of photos of new missile installations throughout the Cuban countryside. Along with the photos taken by Tony's crew, they helped confirm that the Soviets had set up missiles capable of reaching every major city in the US. This was the proof the government needed. The US imposed a naval quarantine of the island and sent four US Navy Carriers to block the entrance to Cuba. An all-out blockade was formed.

Tony and his crew had found out about the plane photographs once they arrived on base at Key West. He feared the situation would delay his retirement. J. P. Moore, director of Perro Negro covert operations, approached Tony after a debriefing.

"Tony, I know you told me that this was your last mission, but I can't promise anything at this point. Things have spiraled out of control."

"But I already put in my request. I'm getting married soon."

"I will do my best, but again, I can't promise anything. I'll let you know as soon as I hear."

It was October 19 when Tony walked into his small apartment, threw his duffel bag in a corner, and flopped onto his bed. He needed to rest and clear his mind before calling Olivia. Seconds later, he fell into a deep sleep.

The ring of his phone startled him. He got up quickly to answer.

"Hello," Tony said, feeling groggy.

"Let's meet." The voice of J. P. Moore was unmistakable, even if his name might have been an alias. To the group, he was *Perro* 1, and Tony was *Perro* 3.

An hour later, Tony was sitting on a bench at Bayfront Park, and someone from the agency approached him. He sat down and offered Tony a cigarette.

"Big Dog wants you to know that he took care of it. You'll be inactive as of Nov. 1."

They talked a while about the current situation and said their goodbyes. Tony left pleased by the news.

Olivia showered and put on her pajamas. She was tired from a long workday and had told Enriqueta she didn't want dinner. She sat in bed towel drying her hair with the door open, as she did every night in case the phone rang. When it did ring, she rushed to get it. It was Tony!

"Olivia, did I wake you up? I just got back."

"Oh Tony, I've missed you so. The news tonight was saying that things in Cuba are bad, and I've been—"

"I'm home now, Olivia. We'll talk in person tomorrow. I love you."

"I'll call in sick tomorrow so we can spend the day together."

"Ok, my love. I'll be there in the morning."

***

Olivia woke up happy. Everyone was gone except her father, who slept during the day in his room. She enjoyed the quiet of those days. No Mari telling stories to whomever wanted to listen. No TV on or radio blasting music from Mari's room. No noise of the pots and pans in the kitchen or cousins coming in and out. Even Gypsy was calmer and napped on her pillow all day. She was having coffee when Tony arrived.

"I've missed you so much," she said as they embraced. "It gets harder every time."

"Don't worry. I have good news. I couldn't tell you over the phone."

"What is it?" she asked, anxiously.

"I will be inactive on November 1," he said with a big smile. "Just a few days!"

Olivia was overjoyed. She made him a hearty breakfast, and they ate and had coffee afterwards.

"How do you like your new name?" he asked. "Olivia del Rio."

"It's like a dream," she answered. "We will be married in less than a month!"

They decided to run errands and left before Lorenzo woke up. They had to get blood tests for their marriage license application.

Tony dropped Olivia off at home that evening and went to see his mom.

Days later, on Monday, October 22, 1962, Olivia was driving downtown for work when she heard President John F. Kennedy on the radio giving a speech. He was informing the nation about the "unmistakable evidence" of Soviet nuclear missile sites in Cuba. He also mentioned the naval blockade and said he had demanded that the Soviets withdraw their missiles. Cubans working downtown went home early that day, and most Cuban-owned businesses closed.

Talk of what might happen consumed the country for days. Tony wouldn't speak on the subject and refused to answer any of Olivia's questions. He just kept repeating, "Give it a few days." But the reality that the Soviets had missiles within striking distance of the US terrified people. The country wasn't safe anymore. People could only ask questions. What was President Kennedy planning to do? What was stopping him from attacking Cuba and dismantling the threat?

During this stressful time, Tony and Olivia had to prepare for their wedding. Tony shopped for a tuxedo, while Enriqueta accompanied Olivia for fittings at Tía Eulalia's house. Olivia decided on a simple boat-neck wedding dress with three-quarter sleeves made of brocade material. She would wear the white lace *mantilla* (head scarf) worn by all the women in her family before her. The mantilla had come from Spain originally, and Enriqueta brought it from Cuba. Tía Eulalia loved the pattern and started working diligently to have the dress ready by November 10, the wedding day.

Olivia was walking on air, and Tony tried to hide how worried he was. Four days later, the inevitable happened. Tony received the call early in the morning.

"The dogs need to go to the vet this afternoon."

He got dressed and rushed to Olivia's house. He couldn't just leave and not tell her, as he had done all the other times. He hoped he was being summoned to base just to share information, but regardless, he had to forewarn Olivia.

"But why do they want you?" she asked fearfully. "You're no longer active."

"I'm still active until November first. Hopefully they just want information for planning purposes." He failed to ease her concern. "It's probably just a meeting, so keep calm. I'll come back as soon as I can."

Tony kissed her passionately, as if to assure her. He felt bad for putting her through this, especially given the timing. As he left, he turned to Olivia and said, "See you later, Mrs. Del Rio. Now go and get ready for the happiest day of our lives."

Olivia stood at the front door waving goodbye and tried to smile, but all she could do was cry.

16

Till Death Do Us Part

Olivia stood looking at all her friends in the middle of a bridal shower at our home. The wedding was five days away, and all she wanted to do was cry. This was my first shower, so I had looked forward to all the spicy games, advice, and stories that people talked about. But Olivia's uncertainty about Tony's whereabouts dampened her mood, and we felt her sadness.

I missed Lucia at gatherings of friends and family. In Cuban households, girls lived with their parents until they left the house as brides. Sisters were meant to be together until then, and having her in New York caused a little pang that never went away.

When people started to look bored, I decided to play music to lighten the mood. I took out my portable record player and suggested that we have a "Twist" dance contest. Everyone liked the idea, or maybe they were just desperate to do anything. "Everyone grab a partner," I said, and I made sure to pair up with Olivia, who looked at me with dread. I started twisting her, and her hips swiveled back and forth. She finally started to smile.

"If we win this contest," I said, "you'll have a story to tell Tony when he gets back."

"Oh Mari, you're too much," she said laughing.

We made it to the final three, but then we bowed out so our guests could win. Two of Olivia's coworkers won first prize. The only problem was that we didn't have prizes! So I gave each of the winners one of my records. Everyone seemed to be in a better mood, which was a relief. Through the din of laughing and talking, I heard the phone ring, and Enriqueta came to get Olivia. By Olivia's sudden look of joy, I could tell it was Tony.

While Olivia talked on the phone, I tried to divert everyone's attention and started a game of charades. People were lively and energetic for the rest of the party. So was Olivia, who returned from her call with a happy glow. I silently thanked God for giving her some relief.

***

As everyone left the shower, Tony arrived to pick up Olivia. He took her for a drive and parked by the bay. Olivia was thrilled to be with him but noticed that he seemed tired and somber. As he spoke, Olivia saw profound sadness in his eyes for the first time ever.

"I've been in meetings and debriefing the last two days because of the missile crisis," he said. "After one of the meetings, they pulled me aside and said they need me." Tony paused and looked at the ground. "They have reversed my inactive status." He said they would still allow a few days for the wedding but that he'd have to leave again afterwards. "I'm very sorry for all of this, my love. If you don't want to get married, I totally understand."

Olivia started crying. "Why is this happening? I thought it was all behind us." She dabbed her eyes. "My nerves can't take this."

"The missile crisis happened, that's why," he said, frustrated. "You need to decide if you want to marry me or not. If there is no wedding, they want me back right away."

Olivia turned from him. She thought long and hard. The pause calmed her down, so she turned back to him. She reached up and held his face in her hands and kissed him.

She gave her answer: "I'll take any time I can have with you."

Olivia and Tony had their wedding on a beautiful November evening. Olivia looked stunning in her dress with a long white train. Tony donned a slim tuxedo in line with the new Continental look of the 1960s and wore his hair slicked back. As they exchanged vows, their voices trembled, and they smiled at each other.

Married at last, they spent their wedding night at The Fontainebleau Hotel in Miami Beach. They planned to honeymoon in upstate New York but knew it would have to wait. They were right. Seven days after the wedding, Tony got the phone call they both dreaded. He left late that same night, while Olivia prayed in their empty apartment.

The next day, she followed Tony's instructions and gathered all their things. She discovered that he had saved her some effort. Tony had already packed most of his clothes, books, and personal items in boxes and loaded them in the trunk of his car. He had also left her an envelope with money, his bank account information, and a key to his safe deposit box along with instructions. *I won't need this. He will be back, and we will take care of things together.*

She got into his convertible and drove back to her parents' house.

Christmas day came, but she still hadn't heard from Tony. The missile crisis was ending, and the Soviets had agreed to dismantle missile bases in exchange for the US doing the same in Turkey. Olivia was sure that Tony would come back any day, and she had worked longer hours so she could take time off after he returned. She decided to wait until then to shop for Christmas presents and all the things they needed. As she waited, and as the days passed, she started to feel sick.

"It's your nerves," Enriqueta assured her. "Why don't you go back to the conservatory? It will do you some good."

"Mami, there is no way I can do that now. Besides, they'll be closed for the holidays."

***

Everyone was worried about Olivia, especially me. She was losing weight and had no energy. One morning, Olivia started vomiting profusely and was so dizzy she couldn't get out of bed. I was on Christmas break and heard her heaving in the bathroom.

"Mami, I don't think it's only nerves," I told our mother. "Olivia might have a stomach virus. Maybe you should call the doctor."

Enriqueta called the family doctor, but none of his advice helped. The vomiting continued, so my mother decided to take Olivia to the emergency room. Mom and I waited for hours in the lobby while Olivia was being treated. Finally, a doctor came looking for us.

"Olivia is resting now," he said. "I gave her an IV for hydration and also some medicine to control the nausea."

Enriqueta looked perplexed and even more concerned. The doctor smiled and patted her arm and then told her not to worry. "She is going to have a baby."

I couldn't believe it! My sister was pregnant, and I was going to be an aunt!

The doctor led us to Olivia's room and brought us inside. She was crying tears of happiness.

"We have to tell Tony," she said. "He needs to know he's going to be a father."

I thought of the happiness this baby would bring her. Thank you, God!

When we got back from the hospital, Tony's friend Julio was sitting in his car waiting for us. The news wasn't good. Word had come from the island that there was a mole in the network. The snitch had provided intel that had led to the arrest of 20 CIA contacts on the island. But the 20 did not include Tony. Still, no one had heard from him in almost a month. Sources passed along that he might be in Boniato Prison in Oriente, where some inmates faced the threat of the death penalty for treason and espionage.

For Olivia, the news couldn't have come at a worse time. She was devastated.

That night we hardly slept. Tony's mother and brother came over to see Olivia, who was desperate and frantic. My mother made Olivia chamomile tea with anise, and she sat under a blanket and stared into space. We tried in vain to call Cuba to speak to any relatives we still knew. They couldn't offer much because they feared for their own lives. So we all sat and prayed a Rosary, and afterwards, Tony's mother left. My father came home from work, and he turned on his shortwave radio where you could hear Cuban radio, but most stations were off for the night. Olivia went outside to sit in the metal shell chair as she had many times with Tony. She looked up to the stars in the clear night sky. *Tony, where are you?* She should have been celebrating the soon arrival of their baby, but instead Olivia was in shambles, while Tony fought for his life somewhere in Cuba.

***

Oblivious to what was going on with Olivia, and without any vestige of hope, Tony lay naked on the damp floor. Deprived of light and unaware of time, he drifted in and out of consciousness. He couldn't see his hands in the dark. He felt feverish from an infected tooth, and the pain of his broken bones prevented him from sleeping. He knew his ribs and other bones were broken, but he couldn't tell which because he ached everywhere. On the ceiling above, there was a tiny hole that allowed in a sliver of sun for an hour or two every day. It exposed the dried blood on his arms from bayonet gashes. Another, slightly larger hole in the floor was for his waste, but he didn't produce much because his meager diet included only worm-infested *harina* and a jar of water served twice daily through an opening in the iron door. He occasionally received a piece of stale, hard bread, but his infected tooth kept him from eating it. The infection had caused him to lose one of his molars.

He wondered how many days he'd been there. Olivia must be worried, he thought. He remembered being chased by the militia after he swam in. Someone must have informed them about the drop-off locations. He had managed to outrun them and eventually found an abandoned cave. After transmitting a distress signal, he was told to go silent and to stay put until support could reach him.

But five days had passed with no food and only a small canteen of water. He was desperately thirsty, so he left the cave overnight to find water. He was drinking from a stream when they caught him and started beating him with the butts of their rifles. Osmany Cienfuegos, better known as the butcher of prisoners and who had ordered the transport of 100 Bay of Pigs political prisoners to be transported in a freezing reefer trailer, in which nine of the prisoners died frozen and asphyxiated, gave Tony's captors orders to deliver him to the infamous *gavetas*, the isolation pits of Boniato Prison in Santiago de Cuba. The last thing he remembered was thirst overtaking him again before he drifted into a deep sleep.

***

Enriqueta woke up early. There was no time to lose. With Christmas holidays and many people on furlough, it was time to reach out to someone that could help find Tony. So far, no one from the CIA had communicated with Tony's loved ones about his well-being, nor did his loved ones know whom to contact. So, she decided to take the reins. She would try foreign connections and consulates first and then follow with the presidents of Panama, Mexico, and, of course, the Vatican. She believed they would offer support, or at least direction. Using the old Olivetti portable typewriter she had bought at the flea market for her studies, she started writing letters. She hoped to put enough international pressure on Fidel Castro to spare Tony's life and wanted it coming from all directions. The first letter was to Fabiola, Queen of Belgium, whose family had lived near Enriqueta's in Cuba. The queen had helped Cuban exiles with worthy causes. Enriqueta was hopeful about that letter and also the one she wrote to the Vatican because of the Pope's repeated calls for peace during the Cuban Missile Crisis.

All the letters carried the same message: "The wife and unborn child of Antonio del Rio implore you to intercede for his life. We believe he is being held in inhumane conditions in the Boniato Maximum Security Prison and has not been charged or tried yet. We fear his captors will execute him without notice or due process."

Her last letter was addressed to US Attorney James B. Donovan. She had read an article in the *Miami Herald* about his efforts to negotiate the release of prisoners from the Bay of Pigs invasion. After typing for several hours, she closed the old typewriter and started to pray.

17

CAUGHT

Olivia woke up every day hoping it was all a nightmare. She knew otherwise, so her mornings were miserable. All she wanted to do was go back to sleep.

Enriqueta remained determined. She came into Olivia's room without knocking and brought a tray carrying café con leche, a soft-boiled egg, and toast.

"Let me sleep, Mami," Olivia pleaded.

"You have to eat this," Enriqueta said. "Now you are feeding two of you."

"But if I eat, I will throw up," Olivia said as she turned to the other side and closed her eyes again.

Enriqueta set the tray on the nightstand and walked out. She put on her sweater, went out into the cool Miami morning and walked a block to the corner mailbox to mail the letters. One by one she put them in, saying a prayer for each. Then she headed back home.

Olivia stayed in her room for hours. Around lunchtime, the doorbell rang, and Mari answered it. Enriqueta heard the voice of a man.

"I am looking for Mrs. del Rio," it said.

Mari paused and then realized he was talking about Olivia.

"Wait a minute," she said. "I will get her."

Mari left to get Olivia while Enriqueta went to the door. The man was wearing a suit and tie and held a briefcase.

"May I help you?" Enriqueta asked. "I am her mother."

"I'm afraid it's something personal, ma'am."

After a few minutes, Olivia came out with her hair in a ponytail and puffy eyes. She looked more like a frightened little girl than the married woman she was now.

Enriqueta moved to the kitchen and out of sight. The man and Olivia sat face-to-face in the living room, while Enriqueta tried to eavesdrop.

"Mrs. del Rio, my name is John Parker," he said.

"Are you from the CIA?" Olivia asked. "Is Tony alive?"

The man didn't answer the first question.

"I'll explain the situation as best as possible. Reports suggest that, as of last week, Tony is still alive and being held in a Cuban prison. We believe it is Boniato Prison in Santiago de Cuba but can't say for sure. Regardless, I am here to inform you that you will receive a check every month for as long as Mr. del Rio is a prisoner. I need you to fill out these papers with your information so that we know where to mail the check. You must also sign this agreement of confidentiality. The checks will come from private bank accounts and will arrive via US mail the first week of every month."

Olivia's mind was racing. *What was going on? Was this man from the CIA? Was his name even John Parker?* She wanted the nightmare to end, but instead it was out of control.

"I don't want money. I want the CIA to get him out of there and bring him back home." Olivia started crying. So did Mari, who was listening and trying to keep quiet.

Olivia composed herself. "I am pregnant. He's going to be a father."

There was a long pause. The man cleared his throat. "I'm sorry," he said finally. "If you have any issues receiving the check, please call this number and ask for me. If I'm not available, provide your name, and someone will call you back within a few hours." Enriqueta peeked around the corner and saw him hand Olivia an envelope. "Here's a check for this month. The January check will arrive soon." He turned and headed for the door without giving Olivia a chance to ask more questions. He let himself out while Olivia sobbed on the couch.

Enriqueta locked the door behind him.

For the next few days, terrible news came from the island. Of the 20 captives, 7 were sentenced to death and executed immediately by firing squad. And in February, they received news that Tony and two more men connected with the CIA would face trial.

Enriqueta called Havana twice and spoke to the only relative she still had there—her husband's great aunt, Estella. Early in Tony's imprisonment, Estella had traveled to Santiago de Cuba to see Tony but was turned away. After that incident, Olivia sent her money hidden in a box of medicines and vitamins (both of which were hard to find in Cuba because of restrictions imposed by President Kennedy in the embargo) so that Estella could find a good attorney to seek Tony's release.

**

The lock of the dark underground cell that Tony had inhabited for three months suddenly began to click. Tony struggled to stand and make his way to the door as it opened. He emerged from his cell squinting in the dimly lit corridor. He was 100 pounds thinner, his skin was mottled with sores and scrapes, and many of his teeth had rotted. When the guards led him outside, sunlight struck him flush in the face and he fainted. They had to bring him inside and try to wake him. No one he knew would have recognized him. His hair and beard reached his midriff, and his naked body was covered in sores and dried blood. All of his bones were visible. When he regained consciousness, he asked a question.

"What day is it?"

The guards laughed, and each of the three gave him a different answer.

He received medical attention and better treatment in the days that followed. His wounds were cleaned, and he was fed decent food. They were preparing him for trial and wanted him to gain some weight. The day of the trial, they gave him a white shirt and pants to wear.

***

The shortwave radio announced the verdict later that day. Tony del Rio had been sentenced to 50 years in prison. It was a miracle, especially when his CIA partner was sentenced to death and was taken immediately in front of the firing squad. Tía Estella told us that, according to Tony's attorney, Fidel Castro had received more than 20 letters from dignitaries around the world imploring mercy for Tony del Rio. When Estella thanked the attorney for saving his life, he responded, "That was a miracle from above. The pressure from those letters was what saved his life."

Olivia had mixed emotions. She was filled with sadness and joy.

"Fifty years," she said. "He'll be over 70 years old when he gets out."

"Just be thankful that he is alive," Enriqueta said. "We will take it day by day."

Olivia was grateful for her mother, who had saved him with her letters. She was in awe of Enriqueta and felt blessed to have her in her corner.

After the trial, the attorney said that Tony would be transferred to La Cabaña Prison in Havana. Worse than Boniato, La Cabaña was a Baroque-era fortress originally built by the Spanish and later turned into a maximum-security prison. It was infamous for *El Paredón*—a thick, long wall riddled with bullets and spattered with the blood and tissue from Castro's firing-squad victims. The young and old perished there and usually without a trial or a verdict; only the orders of Che Guevara were needed. Prisoners were often taken from their cells in the middle of the night and screamed *Viva Cuba Libre!* before gunshots would silence them. People who strolled along *El Malecón* by the seaside at night would hear the shots and shudder.

Mr. Suarez, Tony's attorney, promised my mother he would call once Tony was transferred and would give her a list of needed items. Olivia wanted to send him clothes, medicine, books, and anything that would make his life more bearable. Phone calls in and out of Cuba would be difficult to arrange because callers had to rely on Cuban operators, who were often slow to answer. Making a connection could take hours because lines were always busy.

Things at home in Miami were tense. Olivia kept throwing up and had no appetite. The gynecologist was worried about her weight loss and other effects on her pregnancy. She suffered from severe morning sickness, and any attempt to eat made it worse. She started craving cold drinks, so we would make shakes and fruit juices for her. For protein, she favored ham sandwiches and peanut butter and jelly sandwiches, and that became her diet.

The long-awaited call from Mr. Suarez finally came, and Enriqueta spoke to him at length with a pen and pad in hand. When she hung up, she was visibly shaken. Olivia and I stood in front of her, waiting while she fumbled with the pen and gathered her thoughts. She finally spoke.

"Tony is at La Cabaña prison already," she said. "He saw his father."

"What else?" Olivia asked.

Enriqueta held Olivia's hands. "His father did not recognize him because he has lost so much weight."

Olivia shrieked and then ran to the bathroom to throw up. When she finished and managed to gather herself, Enriqueta told her that he was receiving antibiotics for sepsis. A stronger antibiotic was needed, but Cuba didn't have it. Olivia went back into the bathroom and closed the door.

Enriqueta watched her door close and then took me into the kitchen. She spoke quietly. "Mari, I can't tell Olivia this, but he has been tortured badly. Lost teeth, broken bones, and hearing loss from the blows to the head. He is peeing blood because of damage to one of his kidneys, and they don't know the extent of his internal damage." She began to weep. "Oh Mari, they are barbarians. Olivia can't know how much he is suffering, or she might lose the baby."

"But Mami, this needs to be reported," I said, angrily.

"We need to leave things as they are, Mari. It's bad enough they know he is married to *Esbirro* Solano's daughter. We don't want to make things worse for him."

I wanted to cry and scream. Our brave Tony. How could they do this to a young man? I tried to picture the face of the person who had harmed him, who had caused him so much pain; I imagined the devil with an evil smile. Then I remembered the words of the crusaders for human justice, Dostoevsky and Voltaire before him. One of them had said that "one should judge a society by entering its prisons." How could Cuba do this to its own people?

When Olivia came out of the bathroom, she and my mother both started making calls to pharmacies to ask about the price of the antibiotic Tony needed, according to Mr. Suarez. By the end of the day, they had the antibiotic vials along with more vitamins, an antibiotic cream, shaving cream, toiletries, and some articles of clothing. It was all sent to Tía Estella's house. The Cuban government only allowed medicine and medical supplies, so we feared that the other items would be confiscated (the government opened all packages from the US). We waited to hear from Tía Estella.

Days later, we received a letter from Tía Estella. She had tried to visit Tony but to no avail. He was still in the hospital and refused to wear the prison-issued uniforms, which meant he wore only underwear. He and some of the other political prisoners called themselves *Los Plantados*—the planted—and they rejected uniforms in favor of underwear and refused work orders in protest of their living conditions. Fortunately, Estella managed to deliver the antibiotics and vitamins that Tony needed. The clothing we sent did not make it, so we assumed that whoever had searched the box made off with those items.

During her entire pregnancy, Olivia didn't gain a pound. In fact, by the eighth month, she had lost five pounds, and the doctor was worried. One night in August, Olivia's water broke. She wanted to go to the hospital in Tony's convertible with the top down, "As Tony would have done it," she said. I was the one who drove her to the hospital, so I put the top down. All we could hear down Bird Road on the way to the hospital was the hum of the engine and Olivia's groans.

I protested: "Let me at least close the top, Olivia. We look like two crazy women that have just escaped from a psych ward."

"Tony would have done it this way," she insisted.

By the time we got to Doctor's Hospital in Coral Gables, we were both laughing so hard from our drive that they almost sent her home. But her contractions were well underway, and there was no going back. Before I left the room for her prep, she gripped my hand tightly.

"Thank you, Mari."

I gave her my best hug, and went to the waiting room, where Mami and Papi sat and prayed. Tony Jr. arrived around 5 a.m. Born two weeks early, he weighed under five pounds. Olivia was in labor for about six hours, and then the doctor came out to talk to us. He looked worried, to say the least.

"The baby is here, but there are some issues. He's very small, and his respiratory system isn't fully developed, so we need to keep him in an incubator until he can breathe by himself." The doctor wiped his brow with a handkerchief. "Frankly, it's a miracle he is alive. Most babies that underweight don't make it."

We sat down stunned, not knowing what to do. No one spoke. I went to look for a water fountain and started crying. *When will Olivia's suffering end? How will she take this?* Her baby was sure to bring her some happiness, and here we were, not knowing if he would live.

We went to see Olivia, and she already knew. My father hugged her and started crying.

"Don't worry, Papi," she said. "He is Tony's son. I know he will pull through. Soon he will be home with us, and we will wait for Tony."

When it was time for Olivia to go home, Tony Jr. stayed behind in the newborn intensive care unit. Olivia had never imagined leaving the hospital without him, but she complied with orders. Time without him passed slowly and painfully for Olivia, but finally, after three weeks, the hospital invited her to pick him up. She was thrilled, and I looked forward to meeting my nephew.

At the NICU, the nurses taught Olivia how to suction Tony Jr. if his phlegm got heavy. They also gave her an oxygen apparatus in case of an emergency. When they asked how she would feed the baby, she said with formula, which the doctor had recommended. They seemed relieved.

When the nurses finished instructing Olivia, she completed all the paperwork, and the hospital discharged us. Before we walked out, Olivia turned to me and put the baby in my arms. He was so tiny I could have held him in one hand. "I will love you forever," I told him. "I will always be by your side and help your mom take care of you." I could tell that Tony Jr. would bring hope and happiness to our grieving home. He would change our world for the better.

The day after we brought him home, Olivia asked me to give him his first bath. She told me her hands were shaky, but I think she wanted us to bond. As a family, we were all about making memories, and this one went to the top of my list. Right away, we called him Junior, but I started calling him Juju that day, and it stuck. Olivia liked it, and it caught on with everyone else. The one and only Juju was born without knowing his father's voice but was strong enough to fight for every breath he took.

Lucia flew down from New York with gifts for Juju. When she saw him, she could hardly believe how small he was. Juju stared at her intently before Olivia laid him down in her bed and all three of us sat around him. Suddenly we all started crying. Olivia stopped us before too long.

"We can't feel sorry for him," she said. "He needs to stay strong."

"He is our miracle," said Lucia, "and our love will make him strong."

18

COURAGE

Tony awakened to the sound of footsteps. The darkness of the cell kept him from seeing what was happening. He felt the hands of two men lifting him from the slab and dragging him out of his new cell. Light coming from the exposed bulb in the dimly lit hallway almost blinded him.

"This is the night you die, Antonio," one of the men said.

He had been in solitary confinement since his release from the infirmary. They still interrogated him daily, but he refused to talk. He couldn't tell whether it was day or night or how long he had been in solitary. Sometimes they kept him in a room with bright lights for days, and other days they relegated him to darkness for what seemed like forever. He did know that it was summer because of the heat.

"Walk, Antonio. The *Paredón* is waiting for you."

His heart started racing. *Could this be it? Will I die in front of the firing squad tonight? Are these my last minutes alive? God, don't let me die tonight. I need to speak to Olivia and ask her to forgive me. I didn't mean to leave her this way. Please don't let this end.* The walk to the infamous wall was long and painful. *My father, I heard he was free. I hope he has joined my mother and Robert. I wish I could have known I was dying tonight.*

I would have written a letter to them. Olivia, I love you. You are the love of my life. Under the dim light of a lamp post, Tony could see the six men with their weapons. They faced the *Paredón*, where many Cuban martyrs had died before him. The wall stood at the end of a long courtyard. He had never seen it, but he had heard the shots from his cell many times. He remembered the still moments after the gunfire stopped.

The soldiers stood him up against the wall, while one of them covered Tony's eyes with a cloth.

"No," said Tony, pushing the cloth away. "*Viva Cuba Libre*, you communist bastards. We won't let you take our island."

Tony kept shouting insults at them until they started loading their rifles. Fear paralyzed him, and he suddenly saw the faces of his loved ones flash through his mind. Raising his head up to the star-studded night, he sent Olivia his love. The incomparable sound of gunfire followed, and he fell to his knees. A few seconds went by, and he looked first at his hands and then touched his chest. He was alive! He didn't understand until the laughter started.

Mockery followed: "You fainted, you coward." "CIA men aren't supposed to faint." "Is your underwear soiled?"

Tony had heard of fake executions as a form of torture. He now appreciated the terror it could induce, not to mention how cruel his tormentors could be.

These episodes continued for months, and they made him wish for death. But despite the mental torture and the daily beatings, he wouldn't give in. He never gave them the information that they demanded, nor did he admit to working for the CIA. The only thing his captors learned was that prisoner Del Rio wasn't talking. The *Plantados* planted their feet and stood their ground. No amount of abuse would change that.

***

Junior's first birthday was small, just the family. He was a sweet child with his father's looks and his mother's friendly personality. Lucia and Rick had come down with his parents for their church wedding, which followed a civil ceremony in New York that had taken place months earlier. They had arranged for their Catholic wedding—requested by Enriqueta—to coincide with Juju's birthday. Luci had embarked on a new life and was making a name for herself in New York as a composer, but we were always overjoyed to see her.

Her wedding was simple but touching. As he did for Olivia and Tony, Father Julian married Luci and Rick at St. Michael's Church. Then we celebrated at our house. Lucia played her newest songs for us, and we tried to sing the lyrics. Olivia went to put Juju to sleep and never came out again. She was slowly regaining her strength and her courage, but she didn't want to dampen Luci's wedding with her tears. This day reminded her of how quickly her own happiness had been torn away and occasionally wondered if those moments had just been a dream.

Olivia did get some good news about Tony. Aunt Estella finally had been allowed to visit him, not long after he'd been released from solitary confinement. She gave him the news that he was a father, and his son's name was Antonio Jr. He had covered his head and wept. After he wiped his tears and composed himself, he asked Estella to pass along his love to Olivia.

"Please tell her I love our family and that I wish I could have been there with her."

Estella visited Tony the first Sunday of every month and brought him the medicines and toiletries Olivia had sent. Estella also brought *croquetas* and flan for Tony and some of the other inmates. A few years passed, and Estella finally had the opportunity to leave Cuba on the Freedom Flights, which started in 1965. After she left, little news came from Tony. He was allowed to write occasionally, and that was the only way he could communicate with Olivia. She also wrote to him but didn't always know whether her letters reached him because the prison staff often confiscated them.

Life at home went on without him, and we got used to his absence. Olivia started working full-time at an attorney's office and put Juju in day care. After Tony's capture, she never went back to the Conservatory, and she hardly played the piano. When she did, she would start to cry.

I studied journalism in college and worked part-time at the *Miami Herald*. It was a paid internship, and the work was exciting. Journalism was my passion, and I was one step closer to my dream. My evenings were spent with Juju. He waited for me to come home at night, and I would take him out in his stroller. I treasured these and other happy moments, like when Olivia gave us the news that a famous singer had hired Lucia as a songwriter. Her dreams were coming true, and we were thrilled.

"Mari, let's celebrate with pizza, and I'll buy a bottle of wine."

Olivia went to the A&P to buy wine and then to a pizza place on Flagler Street. She loved Fridays because they reminded her of Tony and their dates. Every Friday he had had a different plan, and every Friday, he had told her how much he loved her.

When Olivia returned home, she opened the bottle of rosé wine and called me over. I had never tasted rosé before. She took out the glasses and poured the wine for us. After clinking the glasses together, we called Lucia on the phone.

"Cheers, Lucia," we said to her. "Here's to our sister the composer," I added.

Every time there was a sister celebration, Juju would clap and jump up and down. He seemed so innocent and carefree. Olivia wondered how Tony's absence would affect Juju. If Tony were around, maybe he would take Juju to football games or teach him how to hit a baseball. Every little boy needed their father, and she knew she couldn't be both parents. Juju had a fascination for airplanes, so we would take him to the Miami International Airport to watch planes take off and land. We would park on a dead-end street behind the airport and watch the action. Juju loved to sit on the hood of the car and point at the planes.

"You see those airplanes?" Olivia asked him. "One day, your father is going to come home in one of them and never leave again."

From that day on, Juju, who, by that time, understood what a father was, would wave to airplanes that flew overhead.

"Is that the plane that's bringing my Daddy?"

"No, not that one, Juju," Olivia answered. "He will come in another one."

***

It had been four years since their wedding. They had spent only seven days together as husband and wife, and she had only received five letters from him since. *I wonder if he still loves me,* she asked herself. *His pillow no longer has his scent, and I'm starting to forget the sound of his voice. What am I supposed to do?* She was a single mom at 23 and probably wouldn't see her husband again. She carried the weight of the world on her shoulders and felt like she was living someone else's life when she had once dreamed of a career in the arts.

It was in the spring of 1969 that Monsieur Lambert called her. He was starting a nonprofit organization that encouraged youth participation in classical music and ballet. They met and discussed the possibilities. Being offered an opportunity to join this effort brought her great hope and a renewed excitement that was missing in her life. Dr. Lambert knew that her family was well known in Miami's Cuban community, and he wanted her to talk to others in the community—both performers and benefactors—about joining the initiative.

"Do you want to join my wife and me as cofounders? Mrs. Lambert will find the voices, and you and I will find the future concert pianists. Also, I have been in conversations with a recent defector from the Cuban National Ballet who might help jump-start our ballet program. We'll have a ballet company in no time!"

His excitement was infectious. Olivia went home smiling that day, but as soon as Juju ran to hug her, she remembered her reality. How could she take on more responsibilities when she had to care for him? Enriqueta and Mari would put her concerns to rest. They encouraged her to be strong and to join the living again.

167

"Don't worry," Enriqueta said. "Mari and I will manage Junior. You can pick him up from after-school care and bring him home. We will handle the rest." Enriqueta would not be denied. "You need this; you were born to share your talents."

Music United Miami (MUM) was formed, and Olivia was given a small office at the conservatory. From there, she contacted everyone she knew, plus any aficionado of classical music and ballet she could find. The foundation quickly surpassed its membership target and had funds to buy more instruments and to hire instructors for underprivileged children. Olivia's life changed; she had a new passion, and now she looked forward to every day. Meanwhile, Junior thrived at school and at home with his grandmother and aunt.

Olivia developed a reputation as an expert organizer of fundraising events. She helped the Kidney Cancer Foundation raise money through concerts and art auctions, which brought her recognition and awards in the years to come. Occasionally, she sat at the piano and played. She played for Tony, who was 200 miles away. But in her heart, he was there, listening just as he did on the day of the competition.

19

The Visitor

Ana waited for a *colectivo*, which could be a car, wagon, truck, or run-down bus with no windows. This time, a truck picked her up and made stops for other passengers before taking her to La Cabaña prison. A long line awaited because it was visiting day. After spending an hour in the sun, her turn came. She provided Tony's name, and the guards searched her thoroughly. The homemade *coquitos* were wrapped in a scarf, and a guard snagged one.

"*Muy rico,*" he said, savoring the coconut macaroons. He pointed her to a bench where she would sit.

Ana thought about Tony and her decision to come. She had considered visiting for months—she found herself thinking about him often—but the trip to Havana from Santiago was almost 12 hours. That changed once she moved to Havana permanently. Her brother Manuel, who had just been incarcerated himself, asked her to check on Tony after she arrived. That was all the motivation she needed to visit a man that had been so kind to her just a few years ago.

Tony was reading the local communist propaganda newspaper—the only thing that the prisoners were given to read—when a guard opened his cell.

"You have a visitor," the guard told him.

Stunned, Tony stood up surprised and tied his shoes. He hadn't received a visitor since Tía Estella almost a year ago. *Who could it be?*

The guard escorted Tony to the visiting area, where he sat down to wait. Another guard brought his visitor to a chair in front of him, and he was puzzled. She looked like Ana, the safe house nurse of Santiago de Cuba. He could tell it was her once she started talking.

"Hello, Tony," Ana said, extending her hand to shake his. She noticed how gaunt he was.

"Ana, it's been years," he said, taking her hand with both of his. "It's so great to see you."

She told him she now lived in Havana because of its proximity to Isla de Pinos. Three of her brothers, including Manuel, were incarcerated there, and she was able to take a ferry ride to visit them.

"Manuel wanted me to come and check on you," she said.

Tony couldn't help but notice she looked uncomfortable. He soon learned why. She revealed that a militia had captured her brother Jose and that he told them about the caves used by Tony and other agents. The soldiers shot and killed Jose nonetheless and then detained her for three days. Afterwards, she abandoned the safe house with her son and eventually made her way to Havana.

Tony was not surprised by the events or upset with Ana. Instead, he made jokes, which put her at ease. They talked about the meals she made and the scarcity of food where she lived with her brothers. When it was time to leave, Ana promised Tony she would return. Tony thanked her profusely and was happy to have contact with the outside world. Ana left the prison relieved and realized how much she cared for Tony.

After that first visit, Ana returned to see him once a month, sometimes twice. On her third visit, Tony told her that he had married and was a father. It was too late by then; she was falling in love with him.

***

The years passed, and Olivia buried her grief and loneliness in her work. Tony's letters had stopped, and she accepted that they would probably not meet again. Occasionally, she would go on a date and feel alive, but it never went any further. Many friends advised her to annul her marriage and start a new life, but she thought of the pain that it would bring to Tony. In his letters, he had said that coming back to his wife and son was what kept him alive. In his last letter, he told her that he'd been transferred to *Combinado del Este*, the newest maximum-security prison in Havana. Conditions were slightly better—books were available to read, and he received more food. He would always end his letters expressing his deepest love for Olivia and Junior.

Junior had a heart of gold and had grown into a responsible young man. His love of family was unique, and I treated him like a son. Not having a father around was the only thing he knew, so he didn't miss Tony greatly. His grandfather Lorenzo—who worked constantly—was his male role model. Lorenzo often told him stories about Cuba and the much-anticipated return. Theirs was a relationship that needed few words. Lorenzo often sat with Junior in the afternoons under the shade of the mango tree and enjoyed the light breeze. Then Juju would watch Lorenzo closely as he lit his cigar. They wouldn't say much; they just seemed to enjoy each other's company. It didn't escape me that Lorenzo was giving up his nap time for the simple pleasure of sitting outside with his grandson. That is the way he showed his love. When Lorenzo did feel talkative, he told Juju stories of Cuba.

Juju used to wonder what powerful force could have made his father leave his mother so soon after their wedding. He stared at their wedding pictures and wondered what Tony was thinking behind that smile. Whenever he heard about his father's frequent hunger strikes, he panicked that Tony would never come back alive. We tried to console him without making promises.

Olivia's job required occasional travel, so it helped that they lived with us. Juju was close to his grandmother and made sure she had everything she needed. Enriqueta had changed since he was born. She was happier and more energetic. She would take care of Junior's every need and catered to his likes and dislikes. Everyone noticed and commented on the transformation. They were inseparable, and Junior, now a teenager, adored her. She never called him Juju though, just Junior or Tony.

As for me, I got the desk reporter job that I wanted and was freelancing at a Spanish magazine. I had a boyfriend named Fernando, but neither of us had plans to get married. He shared my passion for books, classical music, and dogs. Our dog Gypsy had died, and I now had another adopted girl named Coco.

We received word one day that Tony was in critical condition following another hunger strike of the *Plantados*, who demanded medical attention and better food. Olivia thought of traveling to Cuba, but Lorenzo would always stop her.

"The minute you land in Cuba, you will be arrested. Remember the letter that Tony sent you imploring you not to set foot in Havana because they know who his wife is? And they threatened him. Unfortunately, you are cursed with my last name. We are all *Batistianos, esbirros,* and have been declared enemies of the Cuban people." He would plead with her regularly. "Please think of Tony Jr.," Papi said. "What would he do if they arrest you?"

All our family had left Cuba, and there was no one she could send a package to. How she wished she could send him vitamins and medicine.

***

It was Sunday again, and Ana went to the guard house at the entrance to the prison. Her figure was dwarfed by the tall, electrical fence. She carried with her a heavy bag of supplements and medical supplies. She also brought canned milk and bottles of homemade juices spiked with vitamins.

"We told you that there are no visitors allowed, Señorita," a guard told her. "Leave the package, and we will take it inside."

"I want to know how Antonio del Rio is doing," she insisted.

"The strike has ended. They are all in the hospital. Go home and wait for news, Señorita. You are coming here every day for no reason. They will not let you in."

Ana rode the *colectivo* home. Three days later, she received word that Tony was out of the hospital and back in his cell. She sighed with relief. This news meant he had recovered from the physical devastation of the hunger strike. *I will see him in two Sundays on visiting day.* She went to bed and slept for the first time in 10 days.

***

200 miles away, Olivia lay in bed unable to sleep. Tony and the *Plantados* had gone on several hunger strikes, but this one had gotten the attention of the media. Olivia and Juju listened to the Spanish-language radio stations in Miami, and the TV evening news followed the strike's developments. She was so proud of his bravery, and in times like these, she felt that he needed her the most. Nonetheless, her father was right; she couldn't even think of going to Cuba. All she could do was pray that the hunger strikes would get the *Plantados* the help they needed. This one had lasted almost 10 days, but Castro cared nothing for anyone's well-being.

What Olivia didn't know was that Tony's release was secretly being negotiated.

The year was 1978, and a Cuban lawyer, journalist, and activist named Bernardo Benes had been meeting secretly with Cuba to negotiate the release of political prisoners from Castro's inhumane prisons. Cuba was trying to restore diplomatic relations with the US and wanted to change its monstrous image. President Carter, a fierce advocate of human rights, approved secret talks with Castro's government. The meetings had started as early as May, and after five months, President Carter sent Bernardo Benes to Cuba in October to negotiate terms, which included providing Cuba with much-needed medical supplies.

October was a busy month for the arts, because it was concert season for opera and ballet. Olivia worked long hours at her MUM office organizing receptions and writing media releases. *I'm tired, cold, and hungry. I need to listen to my body and go home.* She grabbed her purse, turned off the lights, and locked the building. She got home after 9 p.m. and found Enriqueta and Junior watching their favorite *novela* on TV.

"Hi Mom. How was your day?" Juju said as he hugged and kissed Olivia. "Some man has called you twice today but didn't want to leave his name or a message."

Olivia had an uneasy feeling. *Could it be the Agency? Is something wrong with Tony?* The Agency would always contact her in person. Only twice had they come to the house since Junior's birth; once to inform her of a new payor, and another time to report a change in the return address. The checks arrived punctually every month, and every year the amount would increase significantly without her even asking. No one had her home phone number, and her business cards only listed her office number. Before her mind raced for too long, the phone rang and it was Robert, Tony's brother. He sounded agitated.

"Olivia, I got a call from a man a few minutes ago. He's been trying to reach you because he says Tony is being released along with other Cuban political prisoners, and that he'll be here in two weeks. I was so nervous that I didn't even get his name right. He said someone would let us know the exact date, and that we should watch the news until then."

Robert now lived in Tony's parents' house. Tony's father had been released five years ago and had lived there, but he suffered a fatal heart attack. Then his mom, just a couple of years later, had died from breast cancer. The only member of Tony's family left, Robert maintained a close relationship with Olivia and Tony Jr. and checked in on them often. He held a good job at a bank and was also a wonderful artist. Galleries throughout the city exhibited his artwork at different times.

When Olivia hung up with Robert, she headed straight to the couch where Enriqueta and Juju were watching TV.

"I need to see the news," she said hastily. "What channel are you watching?"

"I'm watching a rerun of *I Love Lucy*," Enriqueta said. "It's the one where she goes for a job interview—"

"Mami, stop. I need to see the news."

Enriqueta complied and changed the channel. The local news showed a picture of Bernardo Benes shaking hands with Fidel Castro confirming an agreement that included the release of more than 3,000 political prisoners.

"Mom, is it true?" Junior asked. "Is my father coming home?" Juju hugged her, and they both cried.

"I can't believe it. Is this really happening?" Olivia said after she had calmed down.

As she lay in bed that night, reality set in. What seemed impossible was now happening. *I haven't seen Tony in 18 years. He has probably changed. What is he like now? What if he doesn't want to be married anymore? Will the seven days we spent together be enough to hold us together?*

She got up to look at herself in the mirror. *I have changed so much. Will I fall short of his memories and expectations?* She was far from the young girl that Tony had left. Her light brown hair was shorter now, and gray hairs were starting to show. Tiny lines now extended from the corners of her eyes and at the edges of her mouth, and her pregnancy had added a few inches to her waistline (although she did still wear the same dress size). She couldn't fall asleep that night. The man who was coming home had been in prison, isolated from society. *What was Tony like now?* So many possibilities ran through her mind. She felt a mixture of fear and overwhelming joy, but she calmed her nerves by deciding that all she needed to do was be ready for him. For the next few weeks, she went apartment hunting and managed to find a nice unit near her family's home. Then came furniture—she picked out a good mattress, thinking he had probably missed that most— followed by sheets, towels, pots and pans, and a dinette set. She decided to wait for Tony before picking out a couch.

The call came on December 10 informing Olivia that Tony would arrive two days later. She was told to go to Tropical Park race track, where loved ones would wait in the grandstands for the newly released prisoners to be delivered from the airport.

**

The night before Tony was scheduled to arrive, my mother, Olivia, and I sat at the dining room table deep in our own thoughts. Junior walked in to join us and seemed nervous.

"Come sit next to me," Olivia told him.

"Mom, I need to talk to you about my dad," Juju said. "I'm worried about meeting him. I don't know what to say and how to act. I don't even know what he's like. You've told me how brave he's been, how he made trouble when he was young, but I don't really know what he's like. I don't even know if he will like me. I'm not brave or a patriot like he is. He doesn't know anything about me." His eyes welled up.

"What's there not to like about you, Juju?" Olivia said. "You are the perfect son. You are smart and funny, with a heart of gold. He'll love you the minute he sets eyes on you."

Olivia hoped her words helped him, but she gave him a hug to be sure. "He's probably just as nervous as you are and is asking himself those same questions right now. But the minute you both see each other, you will be bound by the love of father and son."

Juju nodded in acceptance, but Olivia knew he had more questions and concerns. Olivia was just as worried as Junior was. Tony had been stripped of his youth and now had to be the father of a teenager. Would Tony want to make up for his lost youth or for the years of lost fatherhood? Would he find enough room in his heart for Juju? And not least of all, could they both still love each other the way they once did?

Still, she reminded herself, tomorrow was the day they had all been waiting for. There was no way she'd let her anxiety overcome her excitement.

The morning of December 12, 1978, Olivia and Tony Jr. got dressed early and went to buy flowers to take to the new apartment, a two-bedroom unit just 10 blocks away from Enriqueta's house.

She explained to her son that she and Tony Sr. would spend the first few days there alone to make sure he wanted to live as man and wife.

Olivia arranged the flowers and lit a scented vanilla candle. She wanted Tony to come home to a cozy smell and had heard that vanilla was soothing.

Junior and Olivia arrived at Tropical Park race track at 3 p.m. as instructed. The families of the prisoners waited in the stands. This flight carried the first 70 political prisoners of the 3,000 prisoners to be released. This group included high-priority detainees, including CIA operatives, whose release had been negotiated by the US government. Mari was already there, and she was sitting beside Robert, Tony's brother. Enriqueta decided to wait at home to see if the news would cover the event.

An announcement came over the PA at 3:30 p.m.

"Ladies and Gentlemen, may I have your attention. The aircraft containing the prisoners has landed in Miami International Airport." A wave of applause and cheers followed. People cried and hugged. Tony Jr. leaned his head on Olivia's shoulder. Her hands felt ice cold.

"Don't worry, Mom," Juju said. "Dad will love you again the moment he sees you. Everything will be OK. I'm here with you and so is Tía Mari. You'll finally be together for good."

The event organizers had set up tables with drinks, and Juju went to get us some water.

"Are you OK, Olivia?" Mari asked, noticing how pale her sister was.

"I'm thinking that Tony hasn't seen me for 18 years and might not like me anymore."

"Don't torture yourself. Seeing you and being with you is all he wants."

***

Hours went by with no news. It was 5:30, and the sun was setting. The lights surrounding the track turned on. Someone had arrived from the airport and told us there was a closed-door welcoming committee at the airport for the prisoners but that they should arrive at the track soon. It could be a couple more hours. Two more hours passed, and nothing happened. December weather in Miami is just right; we weren't sweating, but it felt like we were. News came that government officers had released all non-CIA detainees at the airport and that agents like Tony still had to be debriefed, which accounted for the delay. To pass the time, Junior paced the outside of the racetrack. Olivia had no energy and remained in her seat. I decided to stretch my legs and join Juju. Finally, after seven hours—at almost 10 p.m.—a Greyhound bus pulled into the lot and parked close to the entrance of the grandstands. The tired crowd applauded with hope. The bus door hissed open, and several men in suits got out to make way for the passengers. Security had increased without us noticing. One by one, 12 men in suits walked down the steps of the bus and looked around at the stadium. Olivia came down from the stands and joined the families but didn't see Tony.

"He's not here," she said. "I can't see him."

"Calm down, Mom," Juju said, holding her shoulders. "Maybe there is another bus."

Just then, Tony stepped out of the bus and took a deep breath. He lifted his head and looked up at the beautiful Miami night. Only then, did he realize that he was finally home. He wore all white— linen pants, linen shirt, and a white cotton jacket with no tie. His hair was slicked back and his figure was slim. In the distance, he saw Olivia coming down from the stands, and his heart stopped. She was more beautiful than ever. People were speaking to him, but he couldn't take his eyes off her. He realized that Olivia hadn't recognized him. He was much thinner, although muscular, and much of his hair had fallen out. Still, he was the most handsome man who'd come off that bus. He walked closer to her and felt his heart beating wildly.

"Olivia, my love," he said in a shaky voice.

Olivia turned immediately and their eyes connected. There were no words. All the love she had felt for him, all the love that she had struggled to maintain, all the love that she feared she had lost, came crashing down on her like a sudden and unbearable wave. Years upon years of turmoil—fueled by passion, joy, pain, longing—combined in a single moment of recognition. The weight and force of it all made her knees buckle and nearly caused her to collapse. What was real and true, God knew and the rest of us witnessed. Love stormed back as if it had never left. Her man had returned, and there was no turning back just as there never had been. She threw herself into Tony's arms and started crying.

Juju waited a few feet back with me while we also cried. Tony and Olivia hugged, kissed, and whispered loving words to each other for what seemed like an eternity. Then Olivia pulled back and grabbed Juju's arm.

"Tony, this is your son," she said.

Tony stepped toward Juju and embraced him. The three of them hugged, and I joined in. We were a pile of arms, and inside of our huddle flowed a river of tears.

After we finished, we noticed Robert waiting off to the side. He came in and gave his brother a fierce hug. He was too emotional to speak at first. Then he managed the words.

"That is the hug that our mother wanted me to give you," Robert said before handing Tony an envelope. "And this is the letter that our father left you."

Tony's head dropped as he held the envelope against his heart and convulsed with tears.

Back in the car, everyone was speaking at the same time, as Cubans do. Tony looked anxious. Then he asked, "Can you please talk a little slower, I am dizzy. I have heard more conversation today than I have in the past 18 years, and I can't follow what you are saying."

We went to our house where Enriqueta, Lorenzo, and a few of Tony's friends were waiting. Enriqueta had made Tony's favorite—arroz con pollo. But he had been fed at the airport and wasn't hungry. After less than an hour, he turned to Olivia.

"Olivia, where am I going to sleep?" he asked. "I'm very tired."

Olivia noticed he didn't have a suitcase. She asked if he had brought anything.

"Just me, my love. That's all you get after 18 years. I have nothing else but government papers and these clothes they gave us hours before we left Cuba. Castro wanted us to look good for show."

After bidding good night to everyone, they walked towards the car and Olivia asked him if he wanted to drive.

"No, I can't. I wouldn't dare." He looked at a car he didn't recognize. "What happened to the convertible?"

"I tried to hang on to it as long as I could, Tony, but I had to sell it. It was falling apart."

"I should have known."

They hardly slept that night looking at each other and talking. They made love passionately, just as they had on their wedding night. They caressed each other's bodies as if to reacquaint themselves. When their eyes started to close, they forced themselves back awake, and they made love again.

"We need to turn the lights off and go to sleep, Tony," Olivia finally said, calling him under the sheets. "I want to sleep close to you and hold you all night."

Olivia felt like she was dreaming. Right there in his arms, all of her doubts went away. She knew that this was the man she had been in love with and still was. She had tried everything to forget him, wanting to ease her pain. Occasional dates had been a failure. She tried convincing herself that he had chosen Cuba over her so that she could dismiss his memory. She spent 18 years trying to forget him so she could survive, but nothing worked. The minute she saw him, it was as if he had never left. The answer to the question that haunted her was clear: seven days had been enough to last them a lifetime.

The fear of losing him again came to her, and she started shaking. Tony surprised her with a question: "Olivia, do you mind if I sleep on the floor?"

Olivia didn't dare to ask why.

Tony took his pillow and went to sleep on the floor that night. He did the same for many nights that followed.

***

Ana went to the prison to visit Tony on the assigned Sunday. The guards told her he wasn't there anymore and had been released to his family in Miami. One of the guards handed her a letter written by Tony in haste on the back of a prison flyer. "*They are releasing me today. They said my release had been negotiated. I hope they are sending me home. Thank you for all you have done for me. Take care of yourself. Tony.*"

Just like that. The man she loved had left, and all he needed to say to her was written in three lines. He had told her that he was falling in love with her and wanted to be with her in any way possible under their circumstances. She believed him. What was she going to do?

She cried that night knowing she would never see him again unless she found a way to get to the US. How could this have happened? She had heard something about the release of political prisoners being negotiated, but nothing in Cuba ever moved that fast. They always took forever, so she thought she still had time with him. She wasn't ready to let him go. Although she knew how much Tony wanted to reunite with Olivia, she had held onto the hope that someday she would divorce him. She loved Tony with all her heart, but now, with no goodbye, she would never see him again.

20

LOVE WINS

They say that the first year in a marriage is hard. Practicalities and realities of life catch up with you and can ruin your romance. You don't really know everything about a person until you live together. Olivia had been married 18 years, and the man taking a shower in her bathroom was a stranger. The husband she had waited for was a man whose mind was not present. He was broken in more ways than his shattered bones. His state of malnourishment took over his entire being. His soul, his heart, his pride, his ambitions, and even his desire to live had left him. All you needed was to look into his eyes to see his torment. But Olivia was not going to let her happiness slip away. She had found him again and was determined to rebuild anything they had lost in those 18 years apart. And Junior needed his father.

Little by little and with a lot of patience, she started extracting words out of him. Stories of horror and suffering started cascading out. The couple sat through long nights of silence, broken by his stories and, later during sleep, his screams. Slowly, with all the love she had to give, she made him well again. Juju moved in with them after Tony had been back and also showered him with love. Before the month was over, Tony was sleeping with Olivia in their bed and was laughing again. The nightmares continued, though.

Olivia helped Tony find a job at the local community center for the elderly, where Olivia served as a board member. He drove a van that picked up residents, ran errands for the center, and also read to residents with failing eyesight. Slowly, over several months, he integrated into society. Soon, Olivia gave him the news that she was pregnant. It was unplanned, but they both received the news with great joy. This time, he would be at her side, enjoying every minute of the nine months of pregnancy. Tony went with her to as many doctor appointments as he could, which Olivia cherished. When they found out they were having a girl, he wanted to name her Olivia, but later they decided on Cristina.

Cristina came with no complications and brought great happiness to the entire family. Tony would hold Cristina in his arms and stare at her beautiful face in awe for hours. He also started taking long walks with Junior, and they would often go to the movies. He needed to make up for so much lost time. Never in a million years would he have expected this. He had gone from a living hell to having a loving family in what felt like paradise.

They found a house large enough to fit all four of them near Olivia's office. They had driven by the house one day and saw the "For Sale by Owner" sign. The street was lined with royal poinciana trees displaying fern leaves that practically glowed a flamboyant orange. The house had four bedrooms, three bathrooms, and a garage. Juju and Cristina had their own rooms. Olivia loved the large family room with a wide picture window facing the green of the large backyard. Tony planted some fruit trees and took care of the gardening. He kept himself busy and tried hard to forget the ugliness of the past 18 years. The flashbacks still came often and without warning. His vision would blur, and he would start shaking. He tried to keep his anxiety under control so he could function. He needed to forget everything.

Two years after Tony arrived in Miami, Castro, responding to housing and job shortages, announced that all Cuban citizens wanting to immigrate to the US could do so. Cubans left in droves through the port of Mariel and headed for the US. What the US government didn't know was that Castro had emptied his jails of common criminals and mentally ill patients, who now joined the émigrés as "freed political prisoners." Castro's spies also joined the émigrés. Known as the Mariel boatlift, the effort was meant to mock the US. By the time President Carter got wise to Castro's shenanigans and stopped the boatlift, 125,000 Cubans had already entered the US. It was now the job of the CIA to identify the subversives and locate the spies and other unwanted criminals who had dispersed throughout Miami. The ideal choice for the job: political prisoners who'd already spent years in Castro's prisons and knew the political prisoners of Havana's jails well. The CIA formed a special task force to root out Castro's spies, and that's when Tony got the call. The agency brought him in for a meeting and debriefed him about the mission. Without a second thought, he agreed to join the task force.

Later in the evening, after Cristina was asleep, Tony gave Olivia the news that he was on active duty with the CIA again. Olivia was devastated.

"Please don't do this," she begged. "Haven't you learned your lesson?"

"Olivia, they need me. I can't explain what it is, but I won't be in danger, and I won't have to travel."

"Why can't they just leave you alone?" she asked. "You've done your share. And you've suffered enough!"

Her pleas were futile. Tony's sense of patriotism defined him. He had declared war on Castro long ago, and, at heart, he was still a *Plantado*. Since his release, Olivia had tried to get him involved in many things, but he had rejected her at every turn. *Had he been waiting for this?* Olivia felt betrayed and cried all night. *How could he do this again, especially now that he has his children?* Nothing made sense. Nonetheless, she resigned herself to his decision. He had given her no choice but to accept it. That familiar pit in her stomach from years ago was back.

After two days of putting a team together and planning, the task force was up and running, and Tony was walking the streets of Little Havana just as he had many years ago. He felt alive again, with a purpose. He needed the adrenaline that pumped through his veins just as much as he needed oxygen. Olivia had good reason to be scared for him, but the night they argued, he realized that he couldn't change into the man she wanted. He wasn't meant to drive a bus or sit behind a desk and smile at people. Also, anger still burned within him. He had neither forgotten nor forgiven Castro's sins against his family and the Cuban people. He couldn't let the hatred go, and nothing except action could quell it. He had to keep fighting.

Little Havana was the place where the new refugees would mingle and pass unnoticed. They would rent rooms with the small stipend the US provided upon arrival. Some would blow the money on alcohol and women of the streets, while others looked for jobs. Tony and his partner first focused on identifying the criminal refugees and removing them from the streets. Criminals were easy to tell apart from former political prisoners. The former tended to look lost and anxious. The latter had suffered the harshest treatment in Castro's prisons, so they seemed calmer and minded their own business. To avoid detection and to reduce the possibility of violence, Tony and his partner would pick up the criminals in the middle of the night. The overnight detentions helped the agents avoid being recognized. Slowly, the task force started cleaning up the streets of Little Havana, which had seen a rise in crime because of the boatlift. The agents' efforts helped ease local tensions between natives and exiles throughout the city.

The operation would take several years. During that time, Tony cofounded the Ex-Club, a group made up of ex-political prisoners from Cuba. Eventually, he became president of the club, which grew to more than 1,000 members, and they led actions like releasing balloons attached with small gifts and anti-Castro propaganda near the Cuban coast. The balloons would travel into the Havana-Matanzas area carrying scarce personal items—shaving blades, band-aids, and pens—as well as flyers detailing Castro's atrocities and delivering news stories from the outside world.

Whenever he got the chance, Tony spoke publicly about the atrocities he experienced and witnessed in Cuba's prisons. As these engagements became more frequent, and Tony became more vocal, he changed. He seemed obsessive and tormented, and Olivia felt the effects. Increasingly jealous, he didn't like for her to work late and became distrustful in general. Only little Cristina, who was now eight years old, could make him laugh. Juju tried to get closer to his dad, but Tony was remote and uninterested. Although Juju never complained, Olivia could read his disappointment. She attributed Tony's detachment to the weight of carrying so many important secrets. He never told her or anyone what he was doing. She would watch him sitting under the shade of his fruit trees looking so tense that she worried he might be having a heart episode. Every evening, Tony would drink until sleep came. What was once occasional and social drinking became a daily habit for him.

Olivia tried her best to keep peace in their home, but every day, it became harder. Striking up a conversation with Tony was almost impossible. She brought home beautiful stories about the community caring for the needy and about the ways her job was bringing music into the lives of disadvantaged youth, but Tony seemed unimpressed. Junior shared in her excitement, but Tony barely seemed to listen to her words.

Although he was distant at home, his temper could get out of control and reached fever pitch during the time when Olivia was organizing a gala for Opera Miami. She wanted Tony to get a new suit for the event, and he agreed to go shopping with her. They went to Burdines in Dadeland Shopping Mall, where she picked out a splendid gray suit and matching shirt and tie for him. As they walked back to their car, they found another car, unattended, double-parked behind them. Immediately Tony got angry and started honking. When no one came, his anger intensified.

"Relax, Tony," Olivia said. "It's probably someone making a delivery."

Fury blinded Tony, and he could barely hear her. Suddenly, a young man appeared and gave Tony the middle finger. Tony, still in his car, stretched his arm past Olivia to reach the glove compartment. When he opened it, Olivia saw the gun and was shocked. The instant he reached for the gun, Olivia knew she had to do something. Tony's eyes were red, and his facial expression was unrecognizable. Quickly, she pulled down his arm with all of her strength and started yelling and pleading.

"Tony, no! Please don't do this."

"Get off me, Olivia!" he said, furiously.

"Please, Tony, you'll go to jail again. Think of Cristina. She's waiting for you at home. Think of Cristina's face, Tony, I beg you!"

Tony pushed Olivia with his forearm, and her head hit the passenger-side window. As she cried out in pain, he opened his door to get out, but it was too late. The young man was already driving away.

It was all a blur for Olivia after that. They drove home in silence, and she put some ice to the side of her head. The next morning, as Tony was reading the newspaper at the kitchen table, Olivia sat down in front of him. She spoke calmly and to the point.

"What happened yesterday was not only barbaric but unacceptable. I don't know what you are doing with a gun in your car, and I'm sure you won't tell me. But I want you to take it out right now. You could have shot that young man, just because he gave you the finger. You are out of control, Tony, and you need to go to a doctor."

Tony sat quietly looking at the paper. Olivia took the paper from his hands.

"Tony, aren't you going to say something?" Olivia asked. "Why do you have a gun in the car? Don't you realize how dangerous that is?"

Tony got up from the kitchen table without saying a word and walked out the front door. He returned with the gun in its case and gave it to Olivia.

"Here it is," he said. "Does that make you feel better?"

Then he went into their bedroom and eventually got into the shower. Olivia took a deep breath to fight away the tears. She was very worried about Tony, and she didn't know how to help him. *For now, at least, he doesn't have a gun.* It was a small victory but an important one. However, the incident had shattered her peace of mind, and she struggled for the next few days to calm her nerves.

After keeping a low profile at home that week, Tony came home one day with flowers for Olivia to apologize for his behavior. She graciously accepted, and his mood quickly improved. The next morning, he proudly sliced open the first papaya harvested from one of his trees. He served it to Olivia for breakfast with honey and a fresh lime. His face lit up as he talked about watching the papaya grow from a seed, picking it from the backyard, cleaning it, and finally being able to taste it.

Then Olivia, on a whim, asked, "Why don't we open up a nursery and grow fruit trees to sell? You might enjoy that."

"I don't think so, Olivia," he said, his demeanor now serious.

"Why not?"

"Because that's not who I am."

Olivia stayed quiet. She thought of asking him who he was but feared his answer. Instead, she changed the subject to something meaningless.

That Saturday was Valentine's Day, and Tony gave Olivia pearl earrings that morning as a present. They planned to attend a fundraiser cocktail hour for the Florida Republican Party. Olivia wore the earrings to go along with her little black dress. She touched up her hair one more time in the bathroom and grabbed the small clutch she had picked out for the night. Tony looked handsome in the new linen *guayabera* embroidered with his initials at the left chest pocket. When it was time to leave for dinner, Tony couldn't find his keys, so Olivia opened her clutch and handed him her set.

They went to a Spanish restaurant called *El Centro Vasco* that served Spanish-Basque cuisine. Tony seemed happy to be there and, after cocktails, found a table for them. They ordered delicious food matched with an incredible Gran Reserva *Ribera del Duero* wine. Just as they were toasting, they heard someone say: "Tony, Olivia, Happy Valentine's Day."

It was Julio and his wife, and Tony invited them to join their table for a moment. They talked for a while about Radio Marti, a new government radio station that transmitted broadcasts into Cuba. They also talked about the Chain of Democracy, an event where people around the world would hold hands and form a human chain. In the southeastern US, the chain would extend from Key West by boats that would line up all the way to the safest point near the northern Cuban coast. The goal was to bring attention to the many captives still suffering in Cuba's prisons, and Tony had helped come up with the idea. Olivia was proud of him for it and excited for the event to happen.

Julio and his wife didn't stay long because their table became available. The couples said their goodbyes and planned on meeting for dinner in the future.

The evening ended with laughter and with Tony kissing Olivia at every red light on their way home. Olivia thought of the old days when Tony would suddenly pull over and ask her to get out and dance.

As soon as Tony approached their driveway, he noticed a black car with tinted windows parked on the street. Olivia knew something was wrong by the way Tony reacted. He parked in their driveway and frantically told her, "Get out of the car immediately and go inside."

As he did, he reached into the glove compartment for his gun, but let out a curse when he realized it wasn't there. Olivia had tucked it away in the bottom of a drawer in their bedroom. Olivia got out of the car and reached inside her clutch for her keys, but they also weren't there. They were in the ignition. Two men got out of the black car and approached them. One carried a semiautomatic rifle, and the other held a gun. Tony got out of the car and tried to run, but it all happened in seconds. The sound of the bullet burst from the rifle. Olivia screamed his name as one of the men turned his gun on her. She absorbed five shots that slammed her against their front door, and she fell. It all happened quickly and with Cristina and the babysitter inside the house.

21

The Aftermath

Olivia lay on her back by the front door. She could see the blood flowing from her body and running along the brick tiles of the porch. Her arms and legs started to convulse. Behind the door she could hear the voice of nine-year-old Cristina calling out.

"Mommy! Mommy! What's happening? Amelia is scared and is hiding under the bed."

Amelia was the nanny. Olivia mustered the strength to answer her daughter.

"Don't open the door, Cristina. Just get the phone and call 911, like I showed you. Tell them your mom has been shot and give them our address."

"I called them already, Mommy. I want to go outside with you," Cristina came back in minutes.

Olivia was panting and worried she might pass out. She heard the men get in the car and take off.

"Open the door and go to the neighbor's house," Olivia said.

Nothing could have prepared little Cristina for the sight of her mother lying motionless in a huge pool of blood.

"Jump over me, Cristina," Olivia said. "Jump over me and go next door to Maria's house."

Cristina did as she was told. She jumped over her mom's body and landed in the pool of blood. Then she went running to their neighbor, Maria, who was already outside with her husband. Most of the neighbors had heard the shots and had come out to their front lawn. Maria brought Cristina inside and sat her down in a chair near the kitchen.

"Don't worry, your brother will be here soon," Maria said.

Cristina looked down at her slippers. They were covered in blood.

An ambulance arrived and carried Olivia away, while police officers taped off Olivia's yard. Before long, reporters and TV crews were setting up their lights and cameras outside the tape.

As Junior turned the corner on his block and headed toward the house, he saw the lights and the commotion. *Maybe a fire has started in the kitchen*, he thought. The sight of media trucks made him worry. He parked several houses short of theirs and ran to the scene. One of the officers stopped him on the sidewalk.

"I live here," Juju said. "I need to know what's happening. My sister is in there with the nanny."

"The little girl is next door and is asking for her brother," the cop said. "The nanny is being questioned."

Juju noticed his father's car in the driveway. Both doors were ajar.

"Where are my parents?" Junior asked.

"Please come this way," the officer said. "The detective needs to speak to you."

A short man dressed in street clothes turned to shake his hand before pulling out a badge and introducing himself. He was the CSI assigned to the case. Slowly and in a compassionate tone, he relayed what happened. According to one of the neighbors, the black car had been parked outside for a while, and the occupants were waiting for Juju's parents to come home. The detective told Junior about the shooting, about his mom being rushed to the hospital, and his father lying dead in the backyard. The detective said Juju wasn't allowed in the back of the house to see his father's body until forensics was finished.

"Body? He's dead?"

In shock, Junior looked toward his porch and spotted the pool of blood near the front door.

"Where's my mom?" Junior asked, breathless. "Which hospital?"

The detective blew past Junior's questions and instead asked if his parents had enemies. Junior couldn't even think to answer.

He suddenly remembered Cristina. "Where's my sister?" he asked. The detective pointed toward the neighbor's house. Junior rushed over there and found his sister. Cristina was shaking and jumped into his arms. She held his neck and wept.

"Mommy is bleeding a lot," she said. "I think they shot her. There is a lot of blood," she said, still looking down at her slippers.

After reassuring her that she was safe and everything would be ok, he asked to use the phone.

***

When Juju called our house, I answered. Immediately I sensed something was wrong. He launched into an explanation of what happened. He said it all in one breath.

"Tía Mari, can you please come?"

I told my mother to put on the news, hung up the phone, and ran like a crazy person toward Olivia's house. I went straight to the neighbor's house as Juju had instructed. Both he and Cristina were sitting in the kitchen. Cristina sat on his lap shaking. I went straight over and leaned forward to hug them tightly.

"Don't worry, we'll get through this," I said. "The police will catch whoever did this."

That was all I could think of saying. Juju got up and took me to the other room so Cristina couldn't hear.

"Our dad is lying dead in our backyard. I can see his body when I peer over the hedge, but the police won't let me go to him. There's so much blood everywhere!" He paused and ran his hand through his hair. "What happened, Tía Mari? Who would do something like this?" Then he started crying inconsolably. I held him, and we cried together.

"We'll get to the bottom of this, Juju," I said. "We have to stay strong for Cristina."

The neighbor came to us and said that someone should go to the hospital to check on Olivia. "I'm afraid she might not make it."

Juju wanted to stay there with Cristina, so I went to the hospital. When I arrived at the Emergency Room at Jackson Memorial Hospital, the scene was chaotic. Everyone had heard the 11 p.m. news, and many had gone to the hospital. The lights from TV crews illuminated the entrance so much that it seemed like daylight. As I made my way inside, I recognized a lot of familiar faces, but squeezed through the crowd and went directly to the hospital guards to be let in. They carefully verified my identity before letting me inside, and, eventually, I got to her room.

Nothing could have prepared me for what I saw.

Olivia was lying on a stretcher with her head and neck immobilized. A nurse was wiping blood from her arms and face, as someone else in scrubs and a white coat listened to her chest with a stethoscope. Her eyes suddenly opened with a wild look of desperation. She seemed to try to speak but there was a breathing tube in her airway. Tubes were going in or coming out from all over her body. She saw me, and her eyes seemed to want to tell me something, but they closed after someone injected a sedative into her IV. I stood beside her squeezing her hand, but she didn't squeeze back. Her hair was full of dried blood, and I asked for a towel.

"No time for that," the nurse in charge said. "We are taking her to surgery. She is fighting the sedatives we gave her. Before we intubated her, she said that she didn't want to fall asleep until her husband was here. Sorry, we need to get her to the OR immediately. The doctors are waiting.

"I love you, Olivia," I yelled as they wheeled her away hoping she could hear me. "Cristina and Juju are fine."

I sat on a chair in the hallway and began to cry. The waiting room would be full of people waiting to ask me questions, so I didn't want to go there. I started praying, begging, and bargaining for her life. *Why would you let this happen, God?*

Hours passed, and I was joined by Juju. Cristina was with Enriqueta. We held hands and took turns consoling each other's sobbing. After what seemed like an eternity, the doctor finally came out. The operation had lasted more than five hours. The sun was already out.

"She is recovering in intensive care. We were able to remove four bullets but there is one lodged in her neck. Thankfully it seems to have missed her airway and the major arteries in her neck, but the bullet did penetrate her cervical spine. Once she is stable, we will get additional imaging to assess the extent of the damage. For now, you should go home and rest. We'll notify you when she is awake."

We didn't leave. Instead, we found a small waiting room just outside of the Intensive Care Unit where we could check on her periodically. During the wait, a police officer found us. He told us that Olivia would have protection 24 hours a day. The police feared that whoever did this might come back and finish the job.

The next few days of recovery were intense. We couldn't stay with Olivia for long because she became agitated and would try to speak to us. The tracheal tube restricted her ability to talk, and if she became frustrated and pulled the tube, she could damage her vocal cords and trachea. As she suffered through restlessness and pain, the local news reported on the assassination of Antonio del Rio. There were no leads, but the Worldwide Federation of Cuban Former Political Prisoners expressed their belief that the assassins were Castro agents.

An article in the *Tampa Bay Times* described Tony as a former political prisoner who spent 18 years in Castro's prisons. It noted his involvement in both the Ex-Club and the federation of former prisoners, which comprised 1,000 members worldwide. It also acknowledged his contributions to the Tampa Proclamation, a declaration supporting democracy in Cuba, and his efforts organizing the forthcoming Chain of Democracy event. Details of the incident itself were vague. According to Miami police, two men wearing what looked like police or security uniforms had approached Tony and Olivia outside their home. The men fired on the couple, leaving Tony dead and Olivia critically injured. No arrests had been made, but the FBI noted that the attack resembled other acts of terrorism recently perpetrated against Cuban dissidents.

No matter what theories circulated, we knew there was little hope of finding the men responsible for the attack. The assailants were probably long gone, and all we cared about was Olivia's condition. While police officers guarded her room around the clock, our family prayed at the hospital chapel every day for a miracle.

During her long recovery, the doctors confirmed our worst fears. The bullet lodged in Olivia's neck could not be removed safely. Fortunately, it had missed the carotid, but it had severed the cervical vertebrae 4 and 5. The C4 was fractured partially and the C5 completely, which left Olivia paralyzed from the neck down. She was now a quadriplegic but still lucky to be alive. When her condition stabilized, she was moved to a room, and the police stood guard outside her door for almost two months.

Being a quadriplegic is like being trapped in one's own body. There is no choice but to accept dependency on others. Olivia couldn't use her hands, so she underwent intensive therapy to maximize whatever muscles responded. Worse, she struggled to breathe, swallow, and cough. She no longer had control over her body. She had to live without the use of her bladder and intestines, and her lungs barely functioned. She could barely talk because the long period of intubation had damaged her trachea. She had to undergo a tracheostomy to establish a direct airway so she could breathe easier and to facilitate suctioning. A tube was placed in her trachea, and the only way she could speak was to cover the hole with a cork. If she wanted to communicate, we had to "cork" her.

During her stay at the hospital, the staff taught Juju and me how to tend to Olivia's needs, and Olivia learned how to direct her care. The

Jackson Memorial Hospital Spinal Cord and Physical Rehabilitation Unit was one of the best in the country and offered every kind of physical and moral support imaginable. But it was hard, awfully hard, for her and for us. My sister, my beloved Olivia, had become a prisoner of a different sort, and she couldn't even move a finger. Tony had had to bear his imprisonment without her, and now she would have to bear hers without him. Only a strong person like her could endure this test, but even the strongest of humans has a limit.

Juju and I took turns tending to her and tried not to leave her alone. Lucia had arrived right after the accident and stayed for over a month to help us care for Olivia. We all dropped everything to give her proper care, to learn her routine, and to keep her spirits up. My father, who adored Olivia, was having a hard time accepting what had happened to his daughter. Every time he spoke of her, he would start crying. My mother handled her pain in a different way. She was a woman of great faith, action, and strength.

"Crying will not solve anything," she would tell us. "Who says that she will never walk again? What we need to do is pray. The best thing we can do for her is to be strong. We will get her the best doctors, and God will take care of the rest."

One morning, when we woke up at the hospital, she was crying desperately and refused her breakfast tray. She clicked her tongue which was her way of signaling that she wanted to say something. So I inserted the cork.

"Mari, I can't take this," she said. "I have suffered such loss, and I don't want to live like this anymore. The worst part is that I can't even take my life even if I wanted to. I have no hands or feet. I've lost everything, my body and my husband. I need your help."

"Olivia, be quiet, you can't speak like that. You need to be patient."

"Patient? What for? I'll never play the piano again. I can't walk or move any part of my body. I might as well be dead anyway."

She had worked herself up and could hardly breathe. I called the nurse, and she had to be given immediate suctioning because of the secretions set off by her crying. When she was calmer and corked, I took her outside to a small terrace that the rehab patients used to get some sun. I could speak my mind there.

"Olivia, I don't ever want to hear those words from you again. Do you see the blue sky and feel the warmth of the sun in your skin? Do you hear the birds and feel the breeze? As long as you have eyes to see all this and to see your daughter grow up, you are alive! God has saved you for a purpose. Your son and your daughter need you. Many people need you. This tragedy has not taken everything. Tony's killers will be found, and you will be alive to see it."

It took all my strength to tell her all this. Even I didn't believe it. How could she carry on with her life under these conditions?

After I fed her lunch, Olivia fell asleep, and I went to the hospital chapel. It was my turn to cry. I looked up at the empty wooden cross and cried out. *God, why her? Why not me? She is the one that helps everyone. She is the one with all the talent. So many people need her. Why her and not me instead?*

For the rest of her time in the hospital, which totaled eight months, she had no breakdowns and simply focused on learning how to live her new life. During her stay, the Federation of Cuban Former Political Prisoners gave her a courage award. She couldn't attend the ceremony, so she asked me to transcribe a letter that I would read at the event. Juju, Cristina, and I attended the ceremony, where I read her words. They were as inspiring and courageous as she was, especially in her closing.

"My husband was the bravest person I know. So that his death was not in vain, we must carry on for him. The prisoners rotting in the Cuban jails and living unthinkable horrors need to be free. My impediments do not allow me to do all I want, but my dreams walk and travel. I'm with you in spirit, and I am counting on you to continue Tony's work. I am asking you to be my wings."

When Olivia was ready to be discharged, the team of doctors and therapists met with Juju and me to discuss her progress and care plan. We had learned a lot about the life and care of a quadriplegic, but the prognosis wasn't good.

"The life expectancy of a quad with these types of injuries is about ten years," one of the doctors told us. "It all depends on the type of care she has and her will to live."

Juju and I were stunned. This meant that she probably wouldn't see Cristina graduate or marry. To Junior, it seemed cruel; he had just lost his dad and couldn't fathom losing his mom. I could see he wanted to cry. When we left, we swore to each other that she would get the best care possible, and as soon as she got home, he started looking for a live-in caregiver. He was going to find the best no matter what it took.

Thankfully, home meant a new place for Olivia. While she was in the hospital, we found a house next to ours, so Junior sold the old house and moved into the new one. Going back to where it all happened was not an option. Lucia, and I helped Junior pack up the belongings of the old house.

Soon after coming home, Olivia was driving an electric wheelchair. Using the control lever took a while to learn, but she finally mastered it and was grateful for the great gift of wheels. The wheelchair made a big difference in her life and gave her freedom she wouldn't have had otherwise. She called it her wheels, and she could even raise the level of the chair so we could look at her eye to eye. The new house had been adapted to her needs, complete with extra wide doors and accessible sinks. Now, the job was chasing her around in the house. She still needed 24-hour care, but her insurance and Juju's job helped them afford it. After Tony died, Juju had started working at the Ex-Club, the organization his father had started, as an English teacher. He was happy there, and through the prisoners, he heard stories of his dad's courage.

Olivia never went to her office again. Instead, she tried to work from home as much as possible. Little by little, her friends came to visit her, and her social life resumed. She started going to luncheons and community events. Going to the ballet was one of her favorite social events, and in the years that followed, she received several awards for her courage and her service to the community. Juju took her everywhere she needed and wanted to go, and I joined them whenever I could. When the 10-year mark approached, she was healthy and going strong.

22

The Ocean

A year before the shooting, I had broken up with Fernando, and a year, later I started seeing Timothy, the father of the two boys whom I met in my youth during my babysitting days. His name came up after a fellow journalist had written a feature article about his success as a developer. He built high-end homes, and the article was about how his vision had reshaped home construction in Miami.

I got his contact information from the journalist and called to congratulate him. We clicked right off the bat. I had always had a crush on him, but I was a teenager back then, and I had never told him nor did I dare to share my feelings for him with anyone. I heard that he was now divorced and that he had dated afterwards, but he had never remarried. His sons Andy and Eddy were both away at college; his only complaint was that he rarely saw them. After he had given his ex-wife permission to move out of Florida and resettle in Texas, they moved in with her, and seeing them became more and more difficult.

Our relationship started slowly with phone conversations before Tony's assassination. After he heard about the shooting, the conversations intensified. One day, he invited me to a cup of coffee for old times' sake, and then dinner dates. Age had made

Timothy more handsome. He was fit and trim, and his dark hair was showing some gray around the temples. His blue eyes still had the depth and sweetness that I remembered. At first, he wanted to take things slowly. He was scared because of our 15-year age difference, but I was in my mid-thirties and didn't care. I fell hopelessly in love with him. I had never met anyone like him and felt that I had finally found my soulmate. The more we got to know each other, the more things we found we had in common. Being with an older man made me feel solid and secure. There were no mind games, no egos to service, and no lies. The fact that my controversial maternal grandmother Maria Josefa had married a man 20 years older did not escape me. It even emboldened me.

Olivia was worried about the age difference when I told her six months after the shooting, and so was my mother. By then, we had been seeing each other for over a year, and his support during this tragic time helped preserve my sanity. He was the sounding board for all my anger and pain, and he proved that he was there for me unconditionally. The only thing that worried me was that he was reluctant to say he loved me. (My mother worried about other things, like the fact he was divorced, which would keep us from marrying in the Catholic Church.)

I couldn't see marriage on the horizon until he surprised me doubly one night on a dinner date. First, he told me that he loved me madly and had loved me for a while. Then, he got down on one knee at the restaurant and asked me to marry him. I was the happiest woman alive that night. I told him that the day we first met, I lay in bed thinking, *Someday, I'll marry someone like Mr. Collins. Kind and caring.* My dreams had come true.

We had a civil wedding, and I didn't want a big reception, so Olivia insisted on having it at her house. She still hadn't gotten over her reservations about our age gap, but she wanted the best for our wedding. She became alive when she planned events, and this one was very special to her. Olivia also spoke at my wedding, where she debuted her new silver trachea. She had found a surgeon at Mayo

Clinic in Jacksonville who performed a reconstructive procedure on her trachea. We no longer had to cork her, and she was thrilled that she no longer sounded like, in her words, an alien.

Olivia handled her limitations remarkably well. We spoke at length about the little pleasures of life that she missed.

"You know Mari, grabbing my car keys and going out for a ride is what I miss the most," she said. "I miss rolling down the window and feeling the air on my face. I miss everyday things, too, like being able to pour myself a glass of water with plenty of ice and scratching my nose."

Olivia had lost the ability to do the simplest things in life, the ones we take for granted, but she accepted her many limitations with dignity. She made it clear that she didn't want anyone feeling sorry for her.

Juju's support helped immensely. He stepped in as a father figure for Cristina and took care of many of her needs. He still had not married, and most of his free time was spent caring for his mom and his sister. One night Juju, Olivia, and I were helping pick a party dress for Cristina. Cristina finished dressing and looked beautiful. I watched as Juju combed Cristina's hair into a pony tail, and then Olivia broke down.

"What's the matter?" I asked her.

"I wish I could do her ponytail," she said crying. "I haven't touched her hair in so long. The hardest thing is not being able to touch her with my hands and feel her skin and her hair."

The intimacy of a hug and the touch of another human being are primal. Like water is to a flower, a caress is to all humans. Olivia only had feeling in her face and scalp, so she would ask us to put our cheek next to hers. That was her way of hugging. She also loved when we stroked her hair or massaged her scalp. She adored her family and friends and was grateful for every day that God gave her. She showed it with every action.

When I went out to a party, she would say, "You go and dance double. For you and for me. Please dance for us."

When she lacked the ability to do something, she would ask me to "do it for her." It would break my heart, but she didn't allow any tears. She taught us all how to accept.

One summer day, she told us that she missed going to the beach and swaying in the waves. She wanted to taste the salt water on her lips and watch the ocean ebb and flow. When she said that, Juju and I looked at each other and started to plan. A couple of weeks later, we took her to Marco Island and stayed in the same hotel where our family used to vacation. After checking in, the nurse dressed Olivia in her bathing suit and wheeled her towards the beach. Once we got to the sand, her wheelchair sunk, so Juju, Tim and Cristina, lifted Olivia in the wheelchair and placed her under an umbrella. Then we inflated a round yellow raft that we had bought and placed her in it. She screamed with joy as we pulled the raft with the rope and headed to the waves. Cristina and Juju pulled the raft while Tim and I kept her in it.

"Get my hair wet, Mari," she yelled. I took a bucket and poured ocean water over her head. "More, more, don't stop."

She rested her head in the raft and licked the salty waters from her lips.

"I'm so happy!" she kept saying. "I don't want this day to end."

We took her down to the ocean every day for three days. By the time we left, she even had a tan.

***

Three years after the shootings, our father passed away from heart failure. He never got over Olivia's tragedy and would often weep inconsolably. We couldn't bury him in Cuba, as he would have wanted. The man who loved his family, good food, and the ocean—in that order—never saw Varadero Beach or the rest of his beloved homeland again. He had left his island running for his life and was an exile for the rest of it. He worked up until the time of his death.

Eight years later, Enriqueta left us too. Lucia came down during her illness to say goodbye. Our mother died surrounded by her beloved Juju, Cristina, and her three daughters. I never saw a purple sun, but I did encounter what she left behind—wisdom, integrity, decorum, and unparalleled strength.

Olivia continued with her job at the foundation and ballet. From her wheelchair, she moved mountains and organized the best fundraising and charity events in the community. With an assistant by her side, she was on the phone all day reaching out on behalf of the young and the arts, the sick and the poor. She remained involved in all things and efforts meant to oppose Castro. When I visited her, she was always organizing the next event or the next get-together at her house. She was a relentless force for good.

Cristina was thriving and, like her mother, loved ballet. She had become an outstanding ballerina, which brought Olivia great joy. She eventually danced for the City of Miami Ballet Company, and we never missed her performances. We all tried to play matchmaker for Juju, but his dedication to his mother and his job prevented him from taking us seriously. He insisted he would have time for other things later. He had emerged from their tragedy as a pillar of strength and had become the most amazing son any mother could dream of having.

Every year on Olivia's birthday, we thanked God for one more year. The doctors had said 10 years, but she outlived that prediction by a longshot. A full 28 years after the tragedy, Olivia's health began to wane. In her last months, recurring kidney infections took their toll. She would sit outside for long periods watching birds eat at the feeder in their backyard and swim in the birdbath Juju had bought for her. She loved the wind on her face.

I found her there one afternoon with her eyes closed. Gently I touched her shoulder.

"Olivia, you need to eat more and get stronger. You can't go. What would I do without you?"

She opened her eyes and looked squarely at me. "Only God knows when I will leave," she said, "and when he does, you have to let me go. *Dale que tú puedes.*"

At Thanksgiving, Lucia came to visit us as usual, and we all sat around the table joking around, reminiscing, and singing. We sang our family version of "Bohemian Rhapsody" with Cristina leading the vocals. Olivia was quiet and tired that day but also looked peaceful and happy.

That night, after celebrating her 27th Thanksgiving since her accident, Olivia passed away in her sleep. She had beaten the odds. She had won the battle. We let her go.

Years have passed since her death. I miss her more every day as I think of how much she gave to everyone she loved. She left a piece of Olivia inside all of us. Still, I will never be able to fill the void she left.

More and more, I try to think of her achievements and her character more than her struggles. How she served as an example to Lucia and me through our childhood in Cuba. How she helped my father and our family get settled in Miami after we had lost everything. Her devotion to Tony throughout a separation that lasted an eternity. Her commitment to raising two beautiful children mostly on her own. Her success giving young people access to the arts even after a terrible event had devastated her body.

Olivia accomplished more than anyone I have ever known, but my favorite memory of all is still her performance at the Cliburn competition. She played the pieces so magnificently. Those months of practicing and her sacrifice had finally brought her the shining moment she deserved. I am so thankful that we, her loved ones, could see it. She was playing for us then. Just as she played for us all along.

This is my song for Olivia.

About the Author

Maruchi Suquet Mendez is a Cuban-born writer and author of *Finding Home: A Memoir of a Mother's Undying Love and an Untold Secret* (Reedy Press); *Buscando Mi Estrella*, its Spanish translation (Penguin Random House); and the first and second editions of *100 Things to Do in Miami Before You Die* (Reedy Press). She is the co-founder of JunTos Foundation, which helps young victims of heart disease and cancer and their families. She is also a fierce advocate for student-athletes' health. For her efforts, she has been recognized with proclamations from the City of Miami, Miami-Dade County, and Miami-Dade County Public Schools. In 2001, she was the recipient of the American Heart Association's Courage Award.

Maruchi lives in Miami, where she has raised her family and is a proud mother and grandmother.